SCANDAL AMIDST THE STACKS

Dashing Rogues and Ruined Librarians
Book 2

Sandra Sookoo

ARE YOU SIGNED UP FOR DRAGONBLADE'S BLOG?

You'll get the latest news and information on exclusive giveaways, exclusive excerpts, coming releases, sales, free books, cover reveals and more.

Check out our complete list of authors, too!

No spam, no junk. That's a promise!

Sign Up Here

www.dragonbladepublishing.com

Dearest Reader;

Thank you for your support of a small press. At Dragonblade Publishing, we strive to bring you the highest quality Historical Romance from some of the best authors in the business. Without your support, there is no 'us', so we sincerely hope you adore these stories and find some new favorite authors along the way.

Happy Reading!

CEO, Dragonblade Publishing

Additional Dragonblade books by Author Sandra Sookoo

Dashing Rogues and Ruined Librarians Series
Of Dukes and Forbidden Words (Book 1)
Scandal Amidst the Stacks (Book 2)

The Boxers of Brook Street Series
With Love in Their Corner (Book 1)
Go Down Swinging for Love (Book 2)
On the Ropes of Scandal (Book 3)

The Hasting Sisters Series
The Devil's Game (Book 1)
A Second Summertime Courtship (Book 2)
An Impossible Match (Book 3)

Willful Winterbournes Series
Romancing Miss Quill (Book 1)
Pursuing Mr. Mattingly (Book 2)
Courting Lady Yeardly (Book 3)
Guarding the Widow Pellingham (Book 4)
Bedeviling Major Kenton (Book 5)
Charming Miss Standish (Book 6)
Teasing Miss Atherby (Novella)

The Storme Brother Series
The Soul of a Storme (Book 1)
The Heart of a Storme (Book 2)
The Look of a Storme (Book 3)
The Sting of a Storme (Book 4)
The Touch of a Storme (Book 5)
The Fury of a Storme (Book 6)
Much Ado About a Storme (Novella)

A Storme's First Noelle (Novella)
A Storme's Christmas Legacy (Novella)

The Lyon's Den Series
The Lyon's Puzzle
The Lyon's Redemption
Dreaming of a Lyon
The Blind Lyon

CHAPTER ONE

February 7, 1817
No. 10
Manchester Square
Marylebone, London

"Are you going to come over here and converse like a civilized person or are you going to continue to stand at the window, wishing your life away?"

Major Cornelius Montgomery grunted in response to his best friend's complaint. Johnathan Wilmington had always been the voice of reason between the two of them. His hands were clasped behind his back as he, indeed, stood at the window of his drawing room, watching the light snow drift lazily down. Though it was pretty to witness and it covered everything with a pristine blanket that blotted out the ugliness, it made daily life that much more difficult. "That depends."

"On what?" The Earl of Birchfield had been his best friend since schooldays. Even when Cornelius had gone away to fight in the war against Napoleon in the theatres of India, and Johnathan's military ambitions had taken him to Portugal, they'd remained in touch through letters.

"Whether you insist on drinking tea instead of brandy." Now that he had returned from the battlefields with lasting scars, all he wanted was to be back among his men, fighting for a common cause, knowing that he'd at least done something of value at the end of the day.

But instead, he was in London, still trying to figure out how to live his life as a civilian instead of a military man. Yes, he'd been able to rent a moderately sized townhouse in a decent section of Town—the only drawback being that it was quite near to the Seymour Street mews—but it suited his needs. Occasionally, he took public speaking engagements to supplement the income from his pension, but none of it kept his attention or fulfilled him. After a year and a half, the only thing he'd perfected was how to be a rake and entice various beautiful women into his bed.

And then never talk with them again.

Because I'm a damned prick.

The earl chuckled. "Tea or brandy, or brandy in the tea, it matters not." He shook his head, and the candlelight gleamed off the strands of blond mixed in with the brown of his hair. "I merely came for the conversation. It's been ages since I've seen you."

"Yes, well, since I'm not one for the Christmastide holidays, I kept to myself during those weeks, but then I found that hibernation is quite dull." He moved to the sideboard, plucked up a bottle of brandy and two cut-crystal glasses, and then brought them over to the furniture grouping where his best friend sat. "I also don't care for my own company."

"You *are* a miserable sot, aren't you?" The earl took a glass from him and held it while Cornelius poured a generous measure of liquor into the vessel. "It's a wonder any woman can stomach you, regardless."

"My social skills are quite charming, thank you very much, and when I read women poetry, they swoon," he said as he sank into a chair near the fireplace where cheerful flames danced behind an ornamental grate. "Additionally, I only last month bought a closed carriage. Secondhand, but I still own it." That made a difference. Many military men didn't have the means, and living in London was damned expensive. "Also, my talent in carnal affairs is better than most."

"Then what is the issue?" One of the earl's eyebrows rose. "Besides sulking."

"I don't sulk." Much. "I suppose you could say I'm suffering ennui regarding my life. Everything has grown stale." He shrugged then took a sip of the brandy. As it burned all the way down his throat, he relished the odd pain. "When I was in the military, I knew exactly where I was going and what I'd be doing every moment of the day. Now? The days are endless. Full of... nothing of consequence."

"That's understandable. I feel like that as well, and yes, I also miss my days in the military." He blew out a breath. "You and I are different, though, because I have the responsibilities to the title and to parliament." Birchfield frowned into the depths of his glass. "However, I should probably remind you that you aren't getting any younger. Just turned forty, didn't you?"

"Yes, with you coming up right behind me on that age." After tossing back the remainder of his brandy, Cornelius swallowed then winced. "What are you driving at?"

"Well, Valentine's Day is swiftly approaching, and that means there will be a plethora of romance-themed events over the next week or so where many eligible ladies are attending. It would behoove the both of us to make plans to attend at least some of them." He heaved out a sigh. "My mother is constantly badgering me about my unmatched state and reminds me every week that I need an heir for the title."

"Bah." He shook his head. "Love. Something that was invented for fairy stories and to give women hope."

"Because their reality is so horrid?" the earl asked in a soft voice.

"That is the way of things, I suppose."

Birchfield frowned. "You truly don't value women beyond what they can do for you in the bedroom?"

"Of course I do; I just don't want to *marry* one of them regardless of what my own mother wishes." His father had expired while Cornelius had been on the march years ago, while his mother continued bravely on. She resided in their family cottage in Berkshire, where she'd moved when his parents had married. It was where she'd kept house and bore her two children. Though his younger brother had died of a fever as a youth, she kept on as the typical Englishwoman with her head held high. "I know Mama wants grandchildren, but I'm not convinced being domesticated is my path."

"Why? It is one does with one's life."

"Sometimes." He shrugged. "I fear I've been alone for far too long. I enjoy things just so." With a warm and willing companion in his bed occasionally. A man had needs, after all.

"There is that, and no doubt being in the military has rattled your brain. Women aren't keen to marry a broken man."

"I hadn't considered that, but yes, this is so." Cornelius snorted. "What is your excuse?"

A bit of ruddy color rose up the earl's neck. "Don't be an arse, Major. I simply don't wish to marry at this time."

"Why? It's not as if you're a rake like me. Do you have a current mistress?"

"On and off. At Mrs. Simpkins's whim, as it were. She is pouting just now because I wouldn't buy her an emerald parure last week, and I said she won't have it unless she does *something* to earn it."

"Ah, now who is the arse?" Cornelius's eyebrows rose in challenge.

"I deserve that." Birchfield finished his brandy then exchanged the crystal tumbler for a porcelain cup of tea from the service on the low table nearby. "However, I am not interested in marrying. Not because my mistress is so good, and not because I go from flower to flower as you do, but I came home from the war a changed man. Your mental state isn't the only one a bit off, you see." He peered into his teacup. "My perspective has changed in many ways, and now my thinking is coming around to the fact that the English aristocracy is a joke and is rampantly unfair to everyone who isn't titled. I want to change that."

"Impressive." And it took him by surprise. "I respect you for that, but you're facing hills all the way up."

"I know. I'm willing to put in the time and the fight in parliament to pass bills that will help… everyone."

"If anyone can make a dent in the stodgy fixtures in the Lords, it's you. We'll go out and celebrate." While the earl had been sent to Portugal, Cornelius had gone to India. His path had been slightly easier, but that didn't mean he'd not been affected. War was war, and it was hell on everyone. "I believe I once told you that titled men think they're better and they're lazier than men who must hold a position for a living."

"Oh, I'm well aware of that." The earl snorted in apparent amusement. "You think I'm lazy and entitled?"

"I do not. At least not any longer." Sobering, he glanced at the window where the snow still drifted down. "You've changed. You're more pensive, introspective, quiet. You don't flaunt your title or your wealth and keep to yourself."

Cornelius had a feeling he'd changed as well and just didn't wish to admit it.

Birchfield nodded. "Is that a bad thing?"

"That depends." He shrugged. "Are you suffering? Hurting silently?"

"Oh, Cornelius. It's a day-to-day struggle, I think." The earl frowned and shadows haunted his eyes. "Why aren't you? I've found it is difficult to forget the horrors one has seen while in the service of the Crown."

"I never said I wasn't. I just bear that weight differently." Perhaps therein lay the problem. Is that why he insisted on playing the rake all the time when he derived no satisfaction in it, these days? Is that why he was alone at such an advanced age, because he preferred his own company… and that of his demons?

A companionable silence descended on the room, broken only by the snap and hiss of the logs in the fire or the occasional clack of snowflakes against the window.

Eventually, Birchfield stirred, for they'd both been staring into the flames. "Would you like to talk about the things that changed you or still haunt you?"

"I do not." For he feared that once those gates opened, the flood that would follow might prove messy and horrifying. "At least not right now. Do you?"

"No. It's still too close to the surface. I haven't properly sorted it all for my own liking."

Cornelius nodded. "Fair enough." Though eventually he hoped that something might prove a catalyst that would help to rid himself of the traumatic memories.

The earl frowned. "Why don't *you* wish to marry, Major?"

"Honestly? Besides being alone for too long? I believe I'm too broken to subject any woman to what lurks beneath the surface." He rubbed his eyes with his fingers. "Being invited to balls and routs, asked to talk about my time in the military, in India, used to be entertaining for me. But these days, it's just a chore."

"How so?"

He shrugged and wished he were anywhere but in his drawing room. "Society wants the stories. They want the gore and angst. They want their thirst for blood assuaged by tales that feed into their prejudices and fears. As if the killing somehow justifies any of it." A wave of hot anger rose in his chest. No, a year and a half hadn't been enough time away from his military days. "None of that is what really happened in those theaters of war, but my pension isn't enough to live off of, so I take the speaking engagements and pocket the coin. I pay the bills, the rent, try to entertain myself and the handful of mistresses I've had since coming home." He met his best friend's compassionate gaze. "It's not enough to offer salvation, or at least a pardon from the things I've done."

Damn, but he'd never admitted that to anyone.

Slowly, the earl nodded. "You never loved any of those women?"

"I only wanted the physical connection. The rest of me—the

real me—like it or not, is hidden behind walls and locked away, a relic of the past you might say." Through the heated anger, a wave of panic broke, and that terrified him, for what would happen if he released it? "I fear in many ways I don't know who I truly am, these days."

And he'd not been a man he'd enjoyed for far too many years. Since before he'd gone away to war, surely.

"Well, I hope something breaks for you soon that might offer help," Birchfield said, with sincerity in his expression. "Hell, I hope for the same for me." He leaned forward and refreshed his teacup. "In other news, I happened to visit with Penny the other day."

"Oh?" Cornelius's heart beat a tad quicker at the mention of the earl's sister. They'd had a bit of a history together, or rather, there had been the *hint* of a hope of that for him years and years ago, when he'd been younger and foolish. Unfortunately, he'd lost touch with her since the post hadn't been reliable in India, and then once she married, she didn't write as frequently. Whether on her own decision or from a dictate from the marquess, he didn't know. "How is she doing with her husband?"

"You hadn't heard? My sister lost her husband a couple of years ago. The marquess perished in a hunting accident."

Shock slammed into his chest. "I'm sorry to hear that. She must have been devastated." Or perhaps she wasn't. It might prove difficult to tell, since her parents had arranged that particular match.

"Well enough. She's out shopping with Mama this afternoon." The earl shrugged as if his sister's wellbeing didn't matter overly much. "I'm hoping she'll stumble upon a new suitor at one of the Valentine's events this week. She needs to be married, for my mother is anxious to have my future settled. Says it's embarrassing to have both her children unwed without offspring."

Cornelius nodded. "What does Penelope want?" Though her family had always referred to her by her shortened name, he never had, for her given name was far too beautiful not to use.

"I couldn't say. She has only just returned to Town, for she stayed at Weymouth's country estate to help with the transition when his younger brother finally arrived, and the title was transferred."

"Ah, I see. Does she stay with you?"

"No, at Weymouth's St. James townhouse until the new marquess decides to take up residence there. At last I heard, he plans to arrive by month's end or mid-March. Since he'd never planned to become the marquess, he had other interests regarding business."

That made sense. "Shall I call and offer my condolences, late as they are?"

Long ago, before he'd left England for India, Penelope had given him a ring made of her braided hair. It had been a trinket exchanged between him and the young woman who'd sent him off to war with a memento. During that clandestine meeting one summer evening, he'd been a bit in his cups, for they'd all been at Birchfield's country estate—when the old earl had been alive— and he'd met her in the hedge maze on her father's property. There, hidden away, they'd gotten up to scandal with passionate kisses, and she'd let him pleasure her with his fingers and mouth beneath her skirting. Coaxing her into her first sexual release surrounded by the nocturnal sounds under the stars had been one of the memories that had kept him grounded during some of the ghastlier missions he'd been sent on.

But she had always been beyond his reach, destined to marry a man far higher up in society than him. And that night remained a secret between them, for her brother—his best friend—would put a ball in Cornelius's heart if he ever found out.

Birchfield shook his head. "I would rather you did not. I don't want my sister anywhere near your orbit. You're naught but a rogue, and as I've always told you, she is much too good for you."

Damn, so that sentiment hadn't cooled over the years. "Oh,

I'm well aware of that." Equally annoying was the fact that knowing where he stood with his best friend and his sister still stuck in his craw.

Of course, that is what he thought too, yet Penny had been the only woman to have ever made an impression, who had once held his heart in her hands even if she'd never known it. Yes, he'd been the fool half a world away to think himself in love with his best friend's sister, the woman he could never have. When the word came that she'd married a marquess, he'd forced himself to forget about her, to put her from his mind out of necessity. He'd gone on to finish his stint in the military, only having to quit when an injury had sent him home to languish in a hospital for half a year.

Once he finally healed—physically—he had to learn how to meld into society as a civilian, but he'd been forever haunted by that time with Penelope and what might have been if things—if he'd—been different. Knowing she was still far beyond his reach, he'd pulled on the disguise of being a rake, burying his stupid hopes and dreams into that persona, but none of those women ever came up to the mark that was Penny.

"Don't come the crab with me, Montgomery." The earl shot him a cheeky grin. "I've known you since we were children. It is my duty to protect my sister."

"You act as if I'm the devil incarnate, though."

"Aren't you?" Birchfield chuckled. "I've never seen you about Town without a different woman on your arm each month. You have no ambition other than seeing what vice of the moment you can exploit. And you certainly don't have the income enough to keep any woman—let alone my sister—in style."

He put a hand over his heart. "Damn, you certainly know how to cut a man to his quick."

"Can I help it if I want the best for my sister?"

"Even though you didn't oppose her first marriage?"

Another hint of ruddy color went up Birchfield's neck. "That was different."

Perhaps but perhaps not. It didn't matter now. "Well, I'm rather hoping Lady Fowler will be the next to come under my protection. She's known in certain circles as quite adventurous in bedroom endeavors. I could use inventive new ways to get my rocks off."

Since taking mistresses is apparently the only thing I'm good for.

God, what a horrid way to go through life. Yet at the back of his mind, he couldn't forget how hopeful he'd been all those years ago when he had nothing to worry about in life except to wonder if Penny would wish to receive his kisses.

Before the war got to him and changed him forever.

CHAPTER TWO

February 7, 1817
Somewhere in Mayfair

LADY PENELOPE NEEDHAM heaved a sigh as she collapsed backward into the squabbed bench of her brother's well-sprung closed carriage. "Please tell me that we are finished shopping," she said, and if there was a dramatic tone in her voice, she didn't care. They'd visited at least six shops in Mayfair already, to buy things that just weren't needed.

Because her mother had the insane idea of encouraging her—shoving her—back into society to catch a man.

"Yes, of course, but there are a few things I still would like to procure."

"Today?" If she had to "pop" into one more shop, she might act out on the pavement like an over-tired child in leading strings.

"No. It can wait, or I can send my maid to do it." Her mother eyed her from across the narrow aisle as the carriage slowly rolled through Mayfair. A light snow fell outside, which would have made a charming scene except for the conversation. "You know, dear, you shouldn't frown and slouch so much. It plays havoc with your posture and will give you premature wrinkles." Her mother tsked her tongue. "And you're not getting any younger, so you should try to preserve your looks for as long as you can in order to attract a second husband."

"As if two and thirty is ancient." That didn't make her sit up any straighter on the bench. "Besides, I'm a widow, Mama. I don't necessarily need another husband."

"Of course you do, dear. Since your brother hasn't started courting a lady—and doesn't seem to be in a hurry to do so—you are the easier one to marry off, and perhaps then you can start filling a nursery, which wasn't an apparent goal of yours while married to Weymouth."

A stab of pain went through Penny's chest. "I had no control over that."

Her mother huffed as she turned her head to glance out the window. "If you would have let the marquess bed you more often than you did, you would have had at least three children during the course of your marriage."

The heat of embarrassment and anger mixed within her body. "None of that is true."

Her parents had arranged the union between the marquess and her, so at the age of nineteen, she had wed a man who was one of her father's contemporaries. It had been her first marriage, of course, but Weymouth's second. The age difference wasn't the only insurmountable issue in that union. He might have still had his looks, and he had wielded a bit of power throughout the *beau monde*, but when it came to carnal matters in the bedroom, she was destined for disappointment. They only came together physically once a month, and even that hadn't guaranteed she'd walk away satisfied. It wasn't that he was terrible at bedding a woman, it was just that sometimes, he had difficulties maintaining an erection, which had made things horribly awkward and quite embarrassing for the both of them. The times that he *was* able to go through with the act, it was nothing special or even exciting. It just... was. Over the course of her eleven-year marriage, Penny could count on one hand the number of times she'd been sent flying.

And two of those had been by her own hand.

Beyond that? The other disappointment was that none of those couplings had resulted in a pregnancy. Though she suspected the marquess had been sterile—or else his equipage had just been too old—she'd not experienced the joy of having children or being a mother. That theory had been strengthened by the fact he'd not reproduced with his first wife either.

Honestly, when he'd perished in a hunting accident two years prior, it had been a relief to her. Had she loved him? That could go either way on any given day. She had held affection for him borne of familiarity after being in the same household for so many years, but it wasn't the wild, romantic love she'd always read about or heard of from her friends. There were never feelings of drowning in a man or being consumed by him. Over the years, the marquess had become a companion of sorts, a lovely man with lovely manners, raised in a different era so to speak and with ideals that were different from her own.

The sound of her mother's huff brought Penny out of her thoughts.

"It's scandalous that you never had children with the marquess. His title and worth were one of the reasons your father convinced him to marry you in the first place."

"Yes, well, perhaps instead, you should have asked him if his seed was actually viable," she shot off, without thinking. When her mother gasped, Penny waved off the comment as if it didn't matter. "I apologize for the outburst, but you must know that being married to a man who proved sterile was a bit of a disappointment to me."

"For shame, Penelope. Don't speak ill of the dead."

Penny frowned once more and peered out the window at the passing townhouses, brushed lightly with the falling snow. "Well, you certainly didn't wish to hear it when he was alive. You always assumed it was *my* fault. Still do, in fact." She tightened her fingers on the strings of her reticule and gave into a shiver, for it was quite cold in the carriage. The warming brick for their feet had lost its warmth hours ago, for February was always such a bleak month. "And I also won't speak about how he didn't bed me more than once a month in the whole of our marriage, because that might cause you to faint away in shock."

"Why must you be so indecent?" her mother muttered.

"Why must *you* think everything wrong about my marriage was my fault?" She kept her gaze out the window. "Weymouth and I had nothing in common except for Papa. The only thing he loved more than his title and everything that came with it was hunting. All kinds of hunting. I couldn't abide it, thought it barbaric and horrific."

"It is what men with country estates and hunting boxes do, Penny. It's a matter of national pride and luxury."

"It's disgusting." She shook her head. "Be that as it may, I spent many years being lonely in a union I never wanted to begin with. I didn't have the joy of having a Season, of being introduced to society, of dancing or laughing among my friends."

"Yes, because your father and I spared you from all of that. The point of a Season is to find a match. We gave you that, which meant you didn't need society's help." Her mother frowned. "And how ungrateful are you to criticize being handed a marquess who came bearing multiple engagement gifts?"

"I didn't want any of that, Mama." Well, didn't want as much of it as Weymouth lavished on her. So much so that a few times a year, she went to pawn shops all over Town and sold a handful of pieces. Then she donated the money gained to good causes— orphanages, hospitals for returning veterans, homes for the elderly, or groups that taught women from the lower classes to read. "I only ever wanted love and a family." Both of which the marquess didn't give her. Whether he was incapable or it or he simply didn't care, no one would know, and it didn't matter now. He was gone, and she was free.

She gained more love and praise from the causes she support- ed than she'd ever had from Weymouth.

"You'll marry again. I am going to work with your brother to find you a second husband." Her mother nodded and clasped her hands together in her lap as if that settled it.

"*If* I marry a second time, I'll do so for love; I already married out of familial obligation and duty. Quite frankly, I am done with that. If you want more of the same, badger Johnathan." It was time for her brother to have a taste of responsibility, finally, especially since he was the earl now. She was done being bullied by her parents.

"Don't be disrespectful, Penny."

"Yet it's just fine for you to be the same toward me? Making me do things that I never consented to?" She shook her head. "I'm a woman grown who knows her own mind. Since I'm out of mourning, I'm going to do things for me, for my own enjoyment, to chase my own dreams, and if you can't support me in that, so be it."

Even better if some of those things came with scandal attached. She'd been cheated out of that too in her younger years.

"Don't be silly, dear. You are just out of sorts. Once you have a nice cup of tea and some biscuits, you'll be in a better frame of mind to talk about this."

Penny sighed but said nothing, for her mother believed if anyone was having "fits" it was due to lack of tea. Of course, her mother also thought men were the superior sex of the species, and that it was a woman's lot in life to enhance *their* ambitions—personal, societal, and political.

She'd yet to find a man she'd want to sit with her in the quiet times, to support her, listen to her ideas, or to bed her with any sort of authority.

"I don't know about that, but I wouldn't mind the tea." After that, she planned to mope, because it was her right. For too long, she'd had to remain strong and pretend nothing had been wrong. All for the sake of reputations and her image in society.

Her mother shifted on her bench. "It's my hope that both you and your brother will marry before the year's end."

"That's a tall order and one heavily based in fate and luck."

"Be that as it may, I wish for grandchildren as well. Life is far too short to act selfishly and put off these things."

"It's not selfish, Mama, it is merely how life is at times." Except with her brother. He'd had ample opportunities to marry, but since he preferred freedom and his mistress more than responsibility, he *was* acting with selfishness.

It must be lovely to have been born a male.

"Hmph," was all her parent said in return.

The remainder of the drive to the townhouse was accomplished in silence.

Wilmington House
No. 23 Hanover Place
Mayfair, London

MIDWAY THROUGH AFTERNOON tea, Penny's brother came into the drawing room.

"Greetings, Mama, Little Sister." He crossed the room to buss their mother's cheek then sat on the low sofa next to Penny. "I'm leaving for a call and then to my club soon, but wanted to pop in and spend a bit of time with my two favorite people."

She briefly rolled her gaze to the ceiling before landing it back on him. "Do stop. We all know you intend to call on your mistress. Did the two of you work out your squabble?" Her brother never could understand that perhaps he should spend more time with someone instead of lavishing them with gifts, for when the gifts stopped, the people would come the crab.

Of course, he had a terrible habit of choosing the wrong people...

"That is none of your business," he said with a grin, before taking refuge in a sip of tea.

Their mother tsked her tongue. "Enough. We need to discuss the society events the both of you need to attend in order to find appropriate matches."

Both she and Johnathan groaned.

"I'm not willing to marry just now, Mama," her brother said.

"Coming home from the war without my friends was bad enough. I don't need a woman hanging on me with her own problems or adding a child to the mix."

Penny's eyebrows went upward in surprise. This was the first sensible thing she'd heard her brother say in years. "And you already know why I have reticence. Why can we not enjoy Town in the winter and mingle with whom we want?"

Her mother narrowed her eyes. "The pair of you are adamant to try my patience, aren't you?"

"Well, since we both still have free will, I suppose that answer is yes," her brother joked, with a wink to Penny. "And no, the call I'm making this afternoon is *not* to my mistress. She and I are on the outs at the moment, and quite frankly, I can't see that it will end in her favor. Instead, I'm popping over to Major Montgomery's home for a chat and to ask him to join me at my club this evening."

"Oh?" Goodness, but it had been an age since she'd heard that name. While she tried to pretend she didn't care about the man, the hand holding the teacup shook. "How is he these days? I haven't seen him for years."

Though she'd never had a come-out year or any time during the Season to make a sensation, her family had hosted a small ball for her at their country property in Derbyshire. Of course, now, all these years later, she realized it was for Weymouth to come and have a look at her so he could sign the marriage contracts with her father, but she hadn't realized that at the time. The major had been there—he'd been a captain during those days, buying a commission into the military—and he'd been everything blond and handsome.

Eight years her senior, she'd thought he'd hung the stars, and she'd been instantly infatuated with him. He'd always been underfoot because Cornelius was Johnathan's best friend from their Eton days, and he was her first tendre. However, as time went on, he barely ever noticed her as a young lady, and he was much a rake and a rogue, besides.

Yet there had been that one glorious night at the ball, when she'd snuck away for some air and time alone, and he'd come upon her in the hedge maze. Though he was slightly in his cups, he'd treated her to lovely, heated kisses, and then before she'd known what he was about, his hands had gone beneath her skirts. He'd pleasured her private bits with his fingers as well as his mouth, and that had been one of the only times in her life where she'd managed to find sexual release.

Except with him it had occurred naturally, and had felt entirely different than anything gained with Weymouth.

After that, they'd talked a bit of everything except their realities, and when they'd parted, she'd given him a ring made from her hair. Though she'd given it to him in the maze, she'd fashioned it a few days before in the hopes she'd see him. Would he remember that, or had she been just a link in the chain of all his conquests?

Johnathan shrugged. "I believe he's well enough. He needs to mingle more in society, for he's hinted about that he might wish for something steadier in his life now."

Their mother huffed. "If Major Montgomery can manage to become domesticated, that would prove the miracle of the year. He enjoys chasing skirts far too much."

Penny ignored her. "He deserves to have someone who cares for him in his life, the same as Johnathan does, someone who will help to soothe their souls that were damaged in the war."

"It is not polite to mention such things, Penny," her mother chastised. She shook her head. "Is the major even mature enough for marriage? I can't imagine him being happy in a union, for even if he does wed, he won't be faithful."

"You can't say that for certain," Johnathan said with a frown. "However, Penny is correct. He's much like me. Haunted by the war and a bit damaged by it. Any woman he eventually settles on will need to be made of a strong constitution, for he'll need the support and understanding. That is what I'm looking for as well."

Despite the conversation's bent, Penny remained curious.

"Does he have a lady in mind?"

"Oh, I doubt it. I don't fully believe he'll go to that many societal events anyway, but I'll discover more once we have a conversation." He grinned. "Fear not. You are safe from his philandering ways."

That pulled a frown from her. "Why?"

Johnathan winked at their mother. "Cornelius knows you're forbidden fruit, due to you being my sister. Your friends are off-limits as well." He shrugged. "Mama wants you to marry again and to someone high up in society, which you should since you're a marchioness. Someone will snap you up soon, I'll wager."

Not this again. "As if my only purpose on this earth is to be some man's wife or provide Mama with grandchildren?" It would not stop being a sore subject.

"Come down from the boughs, Little Sister." He tweaked her nose, then took a deep draught of his tea. "Of course not, but what else are you going to do? This *is* our world."

The heat of anger rose through her chest. "I *do* work at a bookshop, you know. Eventually, I'd like to run it by myself, perhaps even place orders for the books I'd stock on the shelves if and when Mr. Chandler decides to retire."

"Do stop, Penny." Her mother scoffed. "It's scandalous how you still wish to work a trade. You're better than that."

"It keeps me busy and distracts my mind. I'm a widow and a woman grown. Let me do what I wish with my own life."

"What could you have to worry about, dear? The world is at your feet, and you still have your looks. That means something."

Or it didn't, and it certainly didn't assuage the acute loneliness that assailed her, along with the knowledge that she'd wasted the best years of her life on the dratted marquess. "Regardless, the future and what I do in it is my decision." Though tears welled in her eyes, Penny refused to cry in front of them. "For now, the bookshop is how I'm spending my time, and I enjoy it. Books are never disappointing."

Her mother shook her head. "Well, I want you and Johnathan at the next rout on the schedule. No excuses. There are many debs out there this year you're in competition with and that Johnathan can choose from." She bestowed a grin on both of them. "But you are the real prize, and far prettier than many of them."

Penny snorted. "I rather doubt that. Just as I doubt Johnathan will choose a lady so much younger than he is to take to wife."

"This is quite true." Then her brother stood. He bussed Penny's cheek. "I must run. Behave yourself, and don't deliberately antagonize Mama further."

"Women who follow proper rules rarely meet their dreams." But she waved him off as her thoughts centered on Cornelius Montgomery. What sort of man was he now, and would she find him as appealing and mysterious as she had as an innocent young woman who'd known nothing of the world?

CHAPTER THREE

February 10, 1817

CORNELIUS DIDN'T FEEL much like attending the rout scheduled for tonight that Johnathan had already committed to, and he certainly didn't wish to cool his heels at the club. Additionally, he was between mistresses, and the thought of snapping up the next woman on his list was too much effort. Especially since his last one had begun talk of redecorating various rooms in his townhouse. Which she had only seen twice. That had smacked too much of domestic involvement, so he'd broken things off with her.

She'd thrown a vase of flowers at him on her way out.

Now, here he was, walking through the business district of Mayfair because everything he usually filled his time with sounded so dull and pointless, as if he were existing merely for existing's sake. There had to be more to life than what he currently had.

Hunching further into his greatcoat, he silently cursed the February cold. Ordinarily, he didn't give two figs about the weather, but the chill and frost in the air just sank into a man's bones and made his joints ache to the point that all Cornelius wanted was his fire, a thick blanket, and a bowl of soup.

I have become an old man.

Well, that wasn't quite true. He tightened his gloved hand on the ivory head of his cane. Though he owned three, this one was his favorite. To be fair, he didn't truly need the cane to help him walk; one of the injuries he sustained only slightly inconvenienced him, but he suspected it gave him a sense of security to hold it.

I have turned into an old, grouchy man who wants nothing to do with anything.

He frowned as he passed someone on the pavement. It wasn't such a long walk back to his home in Manchester Square, but he wasn't quite ready to go home just yet. At least he was taking in exercise, and as his mother constantly said—when he wasn't bedeviling him to marry—an idle mind and body were ones closer to the grave. As he strolled, he peered into the windows of the shops that he passed while his breath clouded around his head. Perhaps he needed to plan a trip somewhere, since the war had been over for nearly two years. Somewhere warm with sunshine. Would that help lift the doldrums?

Doubtful.

Since it was nearing the dinner hour, most of the shops had already closed. Pedestrians on the pavement had thinned, but there was still an echo of carriage wheels that rang off the building's facades. Fripperies and fans were displayed in one window while a lovely gown in red satin hung on a modiste's dressmaker frame in another. At a perfumery, ornate and beautiful glass bottles of fragrances had been arranged in the window to resemble the top of a lady's dressing table. An ink seller tried to entice shoppers to buy the latest and greatest in cut-crystal inkwells, while at a cigarmaker, the wealth of accessories and fine cigars was mind boggling. It made him think of lands far away that didn't have winter, where the sun shone down to warm skin and a fresh ocean breeze would rifle through hair.

Perhaps I should shop for a new head for this cane.

At the cul-de-sac at the end of the street, he peered into the bowed window of what appeared to be a bookshop. The wooden sign above the door read "Chandler's Books and Periodicals." It gently swung back and forth in the errant breeze, while a golden pool of illumination spilled from the lit candles within. The place was one of the only shops still open, but he expected the proprietor to close at any moment.

But this window was different, for there was a woman there, arranging stacks of books as well as standing two lengthwise against the stacks. Over the books, she'd draped a string of pink and white paper hearts in homage to the upcoming Valentine's Day celebrations. Finally, she added a cup and saucer of delicate pink ceramic near one of the books. The effect was so lovely, he stopped to stare for the full effect.

As if sensing his attention, the woman straightened. She glanced into his face and happened to meet his gaze. It was difficult to discern the whole of her form since it was backlit from the candles in the shop behind her, but he would recognize the blue-gray eyes anywhere. They had haunted his dreams for far too long, had guided him in perilous times while he'd been away in India.

Penelope.

It was his best friend's sister. As he gasped from the shock, her lips formed an *o* of surprise. Did she know who he was as well?

"Cornelius!" He watched her lips form the word.

So then she did recognize him. Immediately, the old feelings he'd once held for her beset him, and it was as if the years between them had temporarily vanished. A wave of heat slammed into him. He rested a gloved palm on the glass. She lifted a hand, almost touched the glass on her side, but then apparently thought the better of it, for she snatched it behind her back, and what was more, she darted away from the window. Seconds later, she drew a shade downward to block everything within from his view.

With the shade came a sudden surcease to the warm glow of the light from the shop. He stood, shivering in the darkness of the February night, wondering what the devil had just happened. Then, with the knowledge that he might have instantly gone insane, he crunched through the light dusting of snow to the door, put a hand on the latch, and with a deep breath, he pushed the wooden panel open. The cheerful tinkle of a tin bell over the door gleefully announced his arrival.

As soon as it closed behind him, he paused with a frown as he gave his eyes time to adjust the lit room. Why? Did he think to gather courage? To convince himself he was acting the nodcock and that he needed to leave? He tightened his hand on the cane. And what the devil would he say to her after all these years, especially since the last time he'd been in her company, he'd done unspeakable things to her in that hedge maze?

"I'm sorry, but we are nearing closing time. You'll need to come back tomorrow," she said from behind a wooden counter to one side of the moderately sized room where she'd stooped to attend to books on a wooden cart.

A door behind the counter possibly led to a back room where she might find privacy or get a bit of tea while a few wooden shelves to one side of the room had been put together to form a wall of sorts. Two other such "walls" were behind that one, presumably for customers to peruse the stacks as they were.

"I understand that, but I would rather stay and talk with you a bit... to catch up... Penelope." Why he'd dared to utter her given name aloud, he'd never know, but once the words fell out of his mouth, there was no way to recall them.

Once again, she glanced at him, and her eyes widened. "Cornelius, so it was you I saw on the street..." Then she shook her head as if to clear it. "Er, I mean Major Montgomery." She raked her gaze up and down his person, and then she looked again at him with a faint flush in her pale cheeks. "It has been ages since I've seen you."

"Indeed, it has." Where he once prided himself with the ability to charm any woman with witty and risqué dialogue, standing before here, tongue-tied, as if he'd never learned how to speak in the whole of his life.

She pressed the pillows of her lips together, and his gaze dropped to her mouth to stare and remember what those nearly full pieces of flesh felt like against his own. "What are you doing here?"

"Oh, well, I was walking through Mayfair for the exercise. Didn't wish to go home just yet you see. When I happened to glance into this shop and saw you, I…" What? Lost his mind? Was making a cake of himself? Completely forgot he was a known rake in London? He cleared his throat. "I saw you, and since we haven't spoken in some time, I thought to come in and say hello. Offer my belated condolences for the loss of your husband."

"Ah." A frown tugged at the corners of her mouth, and he was far too distracted by those lips then he had the right to be. "Well, uh, what is there to say? Weymouth died two years ago. In a hunting accident. Right before the Christmas season." One of her hands paused on a stack of books on the wooden cart. "Because apparently shooting the hell out of innocent animals is what men of the *beau monde* do as a hobby."

From the annoyance in her tone, it was clear she despised hunting. Not that he blamed her. Too often, men used the escape to their hunting boxes as an excuse to avoid their responsibilities. Personally, Cornelius had never wished to be involved in hunting; he'd had enough shooting and tracking… and killing… in the war.

"Does your brother hunt? Did he go out with Weymouth?" As he spoke, he let his gaze ease over her form with all the familiarity of a lover. Had he been that to her all those years ago? Just barely, perhaps.

The fabric of her dress and shawl seemed expensive. No expense spared by the marquess, no doubt, and the lavender hue hearkened back to her coming out of mourning. Had she cared for her husband once upon a time? His gaze lingered a tad longer on the curve of her breasts and hips. Clearly, she'd come into her own since she'd married. How much effort would it expend to try and charm that bodice down beneath the shawl?

Get your head out of your arse, Cornelius. She is not for you.

"That would assume Johnathan would need to leave London

for Derbyshire." She snorted with apparent derision, and that errant sound yanked him out of his wandering thoughts. "His mistress has too much hold on him, has her claws into him. He's nearly dead but doesn't know it. Frankly, I don't think he's been truly alive since he came home from the war."

Apt description. A grin pulled at one corner of his mouth. "That's about the truth of it. I've said time out of hand the woman's not good for him, but he has his reasons for persisting with her, I suppose." It wasn't because the earl loved her, of that Cornelius was certain. As for the war part, well… The less she knew was probably for the better. "Does that bother you about him?"

"No. I'm old enough to know that's how men are in the *beau monde*." Her shrug lifted her delicate shoulders. "Weymouth was too old for mistresses, at least in a sexual way, but I knew he had one merely as a companion, to talk about things he had in common with where he didn't with me."

That admission was surprising, since Cornelius hadn't spoken to her in years. Perhaps it had weighed heavily on her for the same period of time. Did she have no one in her life she felt close to or could talk with?

"The two of you weren't able to overcome the age difference between you?"

"We did not, and eventually, trying to do so, along with everything else, became a chore. So we let things go." For a brief two seconds, she caught her lower lip between her teeth before letting it go.

He nodded. "Well, I'm sorry for your loss all the same." It was odd, being here with her like this, chatting politely as if they didn't share a history together.

"Thank you."

"No doubt mourning was long and arduous for you." He didn't know all that much about her marriage, only that her parents had arranged it.

"To be honest, I'm glad it's over. My mother expects that I

should continue being broken about his passing, but there was much my family didn't know about my marriage. I'd like to keep it that way." Then she frowned. "Is that all you came into the shop to say? I'd rather not speak of my deceased husband."

Interest shivered through him to crash into surprise. When had she grown into such a forthright, tart-mouthed woman? "What *do* you wish to talk about, then?"

"I wanted to go lock up the shop and go home, but your presence here has turned those plans to rubbish. Mr. Chandler had other matters to attend to today, so I volunteered to look after the shop myself." A ghost of a grin curved her lips. "Eventually, I would enjoy having a bookshop of my own, where I can do what I want within it."

"Such as?"

"Keep the sort of books I adore reading on the shelves. Perhaps offer a tea and chat once a quarter for other like-minded ladies." She shrugged. "I'm sure there are other things as well, but it matters not now."

"Why?" His eyebrows soared. When last he'd known her, she was a mild little miss with a lovely temperament and blushing cheeks and lowered lashes, but now, she was a woman grown who apparently knew her own mind, a woman who had much to say… a woman who wanted to own her own business. It was impressive.

"Why not? I've spent enough years of my life beholden to a man without anything to show for it. Now I'd like to have something of my own that no one can take away from me."

"Fair enough." Which only put more questions about her in front of him. "What would you be doing once home? Nursing a cup of tea with a book in a comfortable chair?" With each word, he came closer to the high wooden counter, and once there, he rested a hand on the polished top. "Or perhaps you have a lover waiting for you in your warm bed?"

"Have a care, Major. That is hardly appropriate," she warned, in a voice filled with outrage as a blush went through her cheeks.

"But no, I don't have man in my life just now, lover or otherwise."

"That's disappointing."

She frowned, but there were questions in her eyes. "Why?"

What the devil was he doing flirting with her? It was beyond foolish, but he couldn't help himself. Those lips were wasted on frowns. "A woman like you should be well-kissed, and as often as she wills it."

"Ah." Surprise shone in Penelope's eyes, and she roved her gaze about his face. "Coming from you, I suppose I should take that as a compliment. Aren't you one of London's most confirmed rogues?"

Is that what she thought of him? And why shouldn't she? He'd long ago perfected that particular image. "No. It is merely an observation from what I'm seeing from you as a grown woman who has life experience behind her."

Surprisingly, she drifted to the edge of the counter on her side with her face a mere six inches from his. "How can you say that, since you and I haven't been in each other's company for far too many years?" Curiosity filled those blue-gray eyes, and brought him right back to that night when he'd compromised her before shipping out with the military.

The faint scent of lilac drifted to his nose, a decided reminder of the summers he'd spent with her and Johnathan at their father's country estate when there were nearly no rules and freedom was at his fingertips. Daring much, he brushed a gloved fingertip along her cheek, and when she didn't shy away, he cupped the whole of her cheek.

"Any woman worth her salt should always have someone in her life that won't hesitate to kiss her as she should be kissed, or how she demands it, regardless of the scandal."

Her eyelids flickered, then her gaze dropped briefly to his mouth. "It's an interesting theory, of course, but a man would need to do something quite impressive in order for me to take notice of him, kisses notwithstanding."

Was that a challenge?

Wanting to find out merely for his own peace of mind, Cornelius moved his hand from her cheek to around her nape, tugged her closer, and then fit his lips to hers. Indeed, they were as soft as he'd remembered. Seconds later, he pulled back. Would she slap his face for his audacity? When she didn't, but instead, peered into his eyes and gave him an almost imperceptible nod, with a soft growl, he fit his lips to hers with more pressure. As he moved over them, she rested the fingers of one hand on his forearm, curled them into the sleeve of his greatcoat, and he couldn't help but chuckle.

Yes, this woman needed kissing, and badly. Had Weymouth not done it enough, or had he been exceptionally bad at it?

Just when he was about to come around the counter, Penelope—or rather, Lady Weymouth—wrenched away with a few fingers to her lips as she stared at him with wide eyes. "I, um…" She shook her head. "You should go. If my brother finds out…"

"Birchfield? Why would he?" he asked with a frown, as an effort to hide how that one almost-chaste kiss had affected him.

She shrugged. "Johnathan oftentimes drives over to escort me home, especially on his way either to or from the Lords."

"Ah." In an abstract part of his brain, he wanted to continue kissing Penelope merely to anger his best friend, but he refrained. "And he's to collect you tonight?"

She nodded. "Most likely."

"Thank you for the warning." There was a certain heat and longing in her eyes he couldn't ignore, but also couldn't puzzle out. Since she didn't encourage another embrace, he didn't push.

Yet that kiss, designed to tease and perhaps annoy her, had made him take a second, harder look at her, and he was ever more curious about the woman she'd grown into.

"Well, goodnight, Lady Weymouth. Have a lovely evening." Then he left the shop with much on his mind.

CHAPTER FOUR

February 11, 1817
Chandler's Books and Periodicals
Mayfair, London

PENNY NODDED TO Mr. Chandler as she came into the bookshop that morning. Then she smiled at Mrs. Chandler, who came out of the back room to bring her husband his typical mid-morning cup of tea and two jam cakes on his saucer. It was a dear little tradition the two had probably indulged in every day over the course of their nearly forty-year union.

I wish I'd had that in my own.

Those little acts of love would have gone a much longer way in winning over her affection—possibly love—instead of being gifted parures of jewelry, expensive clothing made of sumptuous fabrics, or having yet another piece of art installed at one of the properties.

Much of which she didn't inherit anyway. They'd gone to Weymouth's brother.

"Good morning, dear. I trust you enjoyed a lovely night?" Mrs. Chandler, with her mostly graying blonde hair and her soulful, blue eyes, smiled and immediately put Penny at ease.

"As a matter of fact, I did. It was one of the most relaxing I've had in a while." Which had been odd. For the past six months, she'd done nothing but prepare Weymouth's properties and staff for the new marquess. "My brother took me home; dinner was waiting for me thanks to my excellent staff. Then I had tea in bed with a good book."

Of course, that wasn't the only reason, she'd wager. It had been that dratted kiss from Major Montogomery shortly before closing last night. Though he'd been everything lovely and solicitous, there had also been air of curiosity and scandal about him that even now sent awareness shivering over her skin.

Mr. Chandler chuckled. His bald pate fringed with gray hair gleamed in the weak, February sunlight shining into the shop through the front window. "You only need a cat." The sound of his voice yanked her from her thoughts.

"Or a man," his wife said, with a wink and a broad grin.

"Ha! Our Lady Weymouth? She's far too independent," he said, with an equally broad grin. "There's not a man out there who can take her on long enough to marry. She's grown a backbone since we've known her, don't you think?"

"Oh, you dear man. I said nothing about wedding," Mrs. Chandler responded with another wink. "Penny has already had a husband. She should at least have fun now."

The owner peered at his wife over the rims of his half-moon spectacles. "What makes you think she didn't have fun?"

Mrs. Chandler chuckled. "If she *were* and her husband had been worth his salt in *all* the ways that mattered, she wouldn't have taken a position here which keeps her away from home three days out of the week, hmm?"

Before Penny could get in a word, Mr. Chandler set his cup and saucer on the wooden counter with a speaking glance at his wife. "But anything else is rife with scandal."

"A bit of scandal every now and again isn't going to hurt anyone." Mrs. Chandler bustled over the floor. She then flipped the hand-lettered card in the front window so that it read "open" from outside. "But none of this is for us to say. If Penny wishes to have someone in her life, she'll do so on her own time. Not ours or her mother's."

"You two are so sweet." They were like an additional set of

parents she'd never known she needed until she'd met them. "For the time being, I'm perfectly content helping in the bookshop and being surrounded by books."

Of course, memories of that kiss tumbled about her mind at the inopportune moment. She ignored the lazy heat that rose in her cheeks, for she'd probably not see the major again. At best, he'd only been flirting, which was something he was exceptionally good at, if one went by the rumors.

The older pair shared a speaking glance. Mrs. Chandler looked quite troubled, but it was Mr. Chandler who broke the silence first.

"I have been meaning to talk with you about this bookshop and the future of it," he said with a bit of a frown. "Mrs. Chandler and I have bought a lovely cottage in the Cotswolds, to retire there, you see, do a bit of gardening, perhaps get a dog. Been toiling all our lives." He cleared his throat. "I've sold the shop."

"You have?" All her high spirits from before plummeted. "To whom?"

He shrugged. "Some self-made man who wishes to try his hand at running a bookshop. Connected to a lending library, so he'll have a stream of books I don't have access to."

"Oh." Penny frowned as she removed her pelisse of a dove-gray sarsenet. It matched the day dress beneath it. She draped it over the wooden counter. It was quickly followed by the matching bonnet. "When will said gentleman take possession of the shop?" Suddenly, the life she thought she'd have, had been yanked from beneath her feet.

"May first," Mr. Chandler said with a nod. "That's when we're moving house to the country. Do a bit of living before we're dead, you see."

Mrs. Chandler came over the floor and slipped an arm about Penny's shoulders. "Don't fret, dear. And don't look so sad. You can come out to visit any time. You're the daughter we never had."

Her heart trembled, for that was a lovely compliment. "Except you didn't give the shop to me or even ask if I wished to buy it." She pressed her lips together in a frown. "I've been here for years, know every nook and cranny, each book on the shelves. I can list our customers off by heart. I get on well with the men we buy books, stationery, and other wares from. Why wouldn't you consult with me before doing this?" With every word, her heart cracked, for she adored this little shop.

Without it, she had nothing. Especially since Weymouth's brother would soon arrive in London to take possession of his family townhouse. Once that occurred, she would have no purpose except existing.

That all sounds horrible.

"Oh, but dear, you are a marchioness. Running a bookshop is well beneath your station," Mrs. Chandler said with an encouraging nod. "You are meant for better things in this world, I think."

"What is better than having a bookshop being surrounded by books and all the possibilities therein?" A bit of heated panic rose in Penny's chest.

"While I agree, you're still young enough that your mother and brother will see you married to a lovely man, I'll wager."

Penny broke away from the other woman. "When will everyone around me discover that I'm capable of making my own decisions? That, for once, I'd like to do what I think is best for me?" She blew out a breath. "That I might not wish to follow what society deems I should do, or think, or be?"

Mr. Chandler cleared his throat. He bounced his gaze between her and his wife. "I'm sorry, Penny," he said and there was concern and alarm in his expression. "It didn't occur to me to ask you about the shop. I only thought that it would be the gentle urge you needed to put yourself back into society and get on with your life."

Though she wanted to be enraged at them, at everything, she simply couldn't because they were the dearest people she knew. With a sigh, she bussed Mrs. Chandler's cheek and gave her a hug. "Think nothing of it. Perhaps it was a hopeless dream of mine." Because what else was there besides marrying a second time? If she wished to be a mother, that was the only way it could happen. "I would be delighted to visit you in the country."

"Good, good." Mr. Chandler nodded, then took a sip of his tea. "There are still two and a half months here. We'll make them the best. Don't you fret."

"You are no doubt right." She gathered her outerwear and then went into the back room to hang them on one of the wooden pegs in the wall. It had been a foolish dream after all. Yet why were all her dreams so unattainable?

⊱⊱⊱✦⊰⊰⊰

AN HOUR BEFORE teatime, the Chandlers retired upstairs to their private rooms above the bookshop, which meant they would both have their customary nap then enjoy tea afterward. This afforded Penny at least two and a half hours alone by herself in the shop, perhaps three if they slept over their regular naptime, or more if they had errands afterward.

A few customers had come into the shop in the owners' absence, but Penny had assisted them in finding what they'd needed.

Then the bell tinkled as the door opened again, and when she glanced up from a ledger book where she wrote the titles of the books she'd sold, she tamped on the urge to gasp, for Major Montgomery came into the space, looking for all the world as if he had mischief on his mind.

"Oh, Major, back so soon?" That was quite surprising, for after the kiss the night before, she thought she'd made her answer clear.

"I am." He nodded, and there was such an intensity to his brown eyes that she gave into a shiver as awareness crept over her. "I thought to do a more thorough browse of the shop now that daylight has arrived. Just to make certain you have nothing to offer."

"Ah." Not wishing to have him trap her behind the counter as he'd done last night, she quickly scuttled around it toward one of the shelves. "Where can I direct your attention, then? There are many different subjects we have available in the shop."

"While I appreciate that, the subject I am interested in is a bit rare and elusive." As he spoke, he stalked her with determined steps despite his use of a cane, and once again, the determined set of his face set her heartbeat accelerating.

Did he talk about her? Not knowing, Penny popped behind the first shelf, yet he followed her, tracking her as if he were a large jungle cat and she, his prey.

"That might be difficult to find, and I'm not certain it's available in this shop." When he continued to prowl, she retreated around the second shelf.

"I don't mind exploring or digging deep if I have to." As he chuckled, frissons of both alarm and need twisted down her spine.

What the devil is wrong with me?

"I've found in doing so, once the object is finally claimed, that victory is all the sweeter for the pursuit."

Did he truly wish to pursue her, or was he merely interested in a quick tup? And why was she even considering it? "I rather think you'll go away from here disappointed."

"That remains to be seen." Finally, he caught up with her and maneuvered her so that her back was against the shelf. "I seem to recall I was on the same pursuit years ago but was thwarted."

She snorted. "I was young and naïve." No harm in admitting to anything now. "And I was infatuated with you, would have given you anything you'd asked." There was also no use in dancing about their one and only encounter. It was their history.

"Yet I couldn't claim you as I'd wished, for you were to be engaged to Weymouth after that weekend." He narrowed his eyes.

"Were you jealous, Cornelius?" *Oh, goodness, I've used his Christian name without permission.* Why had her voice suddenly become so smoky and low? And why did the clean, crisp scent of his cologne make her feel like she was about to drown in him?

"There was no need to be. I left on a ship two days later." He shrugged. "However, I am here, now, and wish to spend time with you."

"To what purpose? Add me to your vast list of conquests?" When he remained silent, she blew out an annoyed breath. "I'm not interested." *And when have I become such a liar?* "And I'm attending to the bookshop besides."

"More's the pity. Since we are alone, I thought a brief bit of scandal would prove to your liking." His gaze bored into hers. "For you are clearly not the same woman I knew all those years ago."

"Is that such a bad thing?" She lifted one of her eyebrows as she challenged him.

"Not at all." Once he rested his cane against the shelf, he leaned in and cupped her cheek, letting the pad of his thumb scud along her bottom lip. "In fact, it is quite… interesting."

She gave into a tremble. "What do you want, Major? I haven't the time to verbally spar with you just now."

"I wish to see if you are of a mind to let me do wicked things to you, as we did on the faraway summer day at your father's estate."

Was she? Need shot through her core and left delicious shivers behind. "That depends."

"On?"

"Kiss me, and if it is better than your opening salvo of last night, then I'll decide."

"Vixen." He tugged her into his arms, and she went easily enough. How could she not, when this was the man she'd had such a crush on, that she'd pretended she'd married instead of Weymouth?

When he claimed her lips with his, she returned the embrace with the same enthusiasm. It was heaven reacquainting herself with his mouth; the soft firmness of those lips only served to fuel her desire. As he nibbled and nipped, she responded in kind, and once he worried the seam of her lips, she gladly opened for him and touched her tongue to his.

"*This* is the man I remember from that wonderful afternoon," she whispered against his lips. Her fingers curled into his lapels in an effort to haul him closer.

"Then I pass muster?" he asked in a barely audible voice as he skimmed his palms over her curves.

"Yes."

"Good." He continued his teasing, treating her to a series of quick, feather-weighted kisses before speaking again. "I couldn't bring myself to steal your innocence all those years ago; that was your husband's right."

She snorted. "It wouldn't have mattered, except I would have been properly bedded."

Confusion reflected in his eyes. "What does that mean?"

Not wishing to talk about the marquess, Penny tugged at his cravat, making inroads to unraveling the knot. "Never mind."

"Ah, secrets. How delicious indeed." Cornelius drew his tongue down the side of her neck, nibbling and kissing the skin as he went. Flutters chased low in her belly. He grazed her collarbone with his teeth, prompting a tiny moan from her. "Shall I continue, then?"

"Mmm, yes, but if a customer comes in…" A sigh swallowed up the rest of her words when he returned to her lips.

Kisses soon gave way to caresses, and soon his mouth and hands teased her breasts, her nipples through the fabric of her dress, sliding, kneading, torturing. The soft sounds she made at the back of her throat surprised her, but then, it had been ages since she'd been touched as intimately as he was now.

"Oh, that feels so good." Penny hummed her approval and held him ever closer.

Before he could answer, the bell above the door tinkled merrily. Penny froze and frantically met his gaze.

"Call out to them but remain here," he instructed her in a whisper, while pressing her back into the shelf and the books stored there so the person wouldn't see him.

"Penny? Are you working in the shop today?" The exasperation in Johnathan's voice caused Cornelius to grin and her to groan.

"I am, but I am assisting a customer at the moment. I'll be right there."

"Not if I have anything to say about it," Cornelius said in a barely there whisper. Then, he spun her about and kneeled at her feet. When she threw a questioning glance over her shoulder, he winked and then encouraged her legs apart.

Oh, dear Lord. "What are you about?" she asked silently. Surely, he didn't mean to…

"You'll find out in a moment," he mouthed back.

The earl cleared his throat. "Listen, Sis, we need to discuss your promise that you'll attend the events leading up to Valentine's Day this week. Mama is adamant that you meet someone and bring him up to scratch by year's end." A hint of annoyance bordering on arrogance rang in his voice. "I grow weary of being her watchdog."

"She wants the same from you, so why should I follow orders if you won't?

"Perhaps I don't want you to land in another arranged marriage."

Penny frowned and peered through the books, hoping her brother didn't advance. "You thought Mama and Papa were wrong to foist Weymouth upon me?" He'd never talked about it with her before.

"I didn't at the time."

Cornelius slowly, silently shoved her skirting up and asked her silently to hold the fabric out of his way. Then he dared to trail his fingertips along the inside of her thigh and gave the same treatment to the other.

"And now?" Penny's response was on the breathless side. Her skin quivered beneath Cornelius's fingertips. Tiny dots of gooseflesh rose at his touch.

"I believe you were given a bad deal. Whispers around the clubs held that Weymouth wasn't exactly… gifted in the bedroom arts."

Heat slapped her cheeks. "Oh." Had she been gossiped about by gentlemen about Town? "Did you indulge in that sort of talk as well?"

"Of course not, but was it true?"

"I'd rather not say." Especially not with Cornelius right there.

While she talked with her brother, the major drew abstract designs on her inner thigh and moved his fingertips upward to caress her folds. The touch was so unexpected that she was obliged to stifle a gasp. As he blew a breath over one exposed arse cheek, he stood and fit his hand more fully to that secret flesh between her thighs.

"Are you out of your mind?" she hissed in a barely audible voice.

"That largely depends on the day," he whispered back.

The sound of footsteps stopped as Johnathan reached the first shelf. "Fair enough, but don't you miss being married?" A certain hopefulness had entered his voice. "Now that I'm the earl, I want to see you settled so I don't need to worry."

Her heart squeezed. "Perhaps I wish to become one of those independently wealthy widows who does what she will." Penny gasped but squirmed from Cornelius's continued attentions. How could she continue conversing when the major's fingers on her person would slowly steal her facilities? "I enjoy my freedom too much." Her voice quavered with each strum of his fingers on her folds.

Johnathan snorted. "You can have your freedom while being cared for and settled."

"And have a husband take over my properties or my coin? No, thank you." She shook her head and then bit her lip when Cornelius rubbed the pad of his forefinger over the swollen nubbin at her center. How was it possible he could bring her so near to a release when he'd barely touched her?

"There is that, but don't put yourself on the shelf merely for that. Don't you want to be a mother?"

A strangled sound left Penny's throat, whether from her brother's words or Cornelius's constant friction on her nubbin, she couldn't say. "Yes, of course, but…"

"Yet you balk at the idea of marriage. You won't change your mind?"

Cornelius again went onto his knees. He put his mouth on her, flicking his tongue over her swollen bundle of nerves where his fingers had just been.

"No!" The exclamation echoed in the room. Penny dropped a hand on Cornelius's shoulder and dug in her fingers. Did the man have no shame?

He met her gaze with a grin and continued his torment.

"Well, you needn't be so vehement about it," Johnathan said, his tone petulant. "I merely want to see you cared for."

"So I don't become your responsibility, you mean?" she asked with a trace of hysteria in her voice.

Cornelius continued to pleasure her as if his life depended upon bringing her to completion in the next few moments.

"Don't be like that, Penny. It something were to happen to me, I want to go into the Great Beyond knowing someone will take care of you."

"Are you ill?" What did he refer to? Somewhat concerned, yet unable to concentrate, she held the major's head with one hand while clutching her skirts to her chest with the other.

"Not in the traditional sense."

She frowned. "The demons from the war?"

"Perhaps, so please, for both our sakes, find someone you can rub along with."

"Stop trying to order me about. My only concern at the moment is finding satisfaction here at the bookshop." That last word was drawn out on a moan.

Johnathan took a few steps forward. "Are you quite all right, Sis?"

"Yes! Just helping a customer." Breathless, she'd thrown back her head. A couple of pins fell from her hair, and the heavy caramel-blonde tresses tumbled about her shoulders. With labored breathing, she slowly moved, bumping against the major's mouth, but Cornelius grasped her hips, holding her still.

The wicked man sucked and teased that button for all he was worth, first using strong friction and then following with gentle, soothing licks to keep her on that edge.

"Penny? Do you require assistance back there?"

"No, I'm doing quite well. Delicious, in fact," she gasped out. "Saw a spider, that's all.

"Horrid beasties."

She could almost hear her brother nod. The situation was most amusing and somewhat surreal. What would Johnathan say if he knew his best friend was pleasuring her while he was in the room? At the moment, Penny didn't care, for they'd passed both wicked and proper already. The major continued to dance his fingers over her skin. Knowing there was nothing she could do about the present situation and knowing also that her brother was clueless, she stifled a cry when Cornelius lifted a hand and rolled one of her nipples, alternating that sensation with a series of sharp pinches that had her sagging in his hold.

"Oh, God," she whispered, trying hard to stifle any sound with her eyes shuttered.

Johnathan, damn his eyes, continued his stilted conversation. "Those damned things make me go squeamish immediately."

"Oh, yes." She talked exclusively to the major, her body trembling, her fingers flexing on his shoulder. Any minute she'd fall into release, and if her deuced brother didn't leave, they'd all end up embarrassed. "Go… away…" she panted.

"You're obviously… involved in your work." Johnathan cleared his throat. "Will I drive you to the Fortners' rout tonight?"

"I cannot wait!" She was near frantic, her whole body thrusting against the major's hand, and Cornelius didn't let up.

"No need to make jest of it, sis. If I didn't know better, I'd say *your* mind is beginning to go unhinged instead of mine." Johnathan's footsteps echoed on the hardwood as he crossed the room. "Don't dawdle when your butler tells you my carriage is outside. Mama and I will need you to come quickly."

"I'm endeavoring to do just that," she whispered, trembling in Cornelius's hold.

"By the by, I don't like this new, independent attitude of yours." But her brother finally left and the tin bell over the door tinkled.

When the door snicked closed, Cornelius paused in his ministrations and glanced up at her. "Your composure under pressure is admirable."

"The pair of you need to be damned for all eternity." She tossed her head. Heat slapped at her cheeks. "Finish me. I'm nearly done." Was that too waspish of a command?

"Damn, I rather like your tart mouth." He resumed his task, adding extra tension and friction with his fingers as he worked her over with his tongue and teeth.

"Oh, oh!" Penny undulated her hips, held his head to her body, and when he increased his suction, she hit release and shattered in spectacular fashion. Bliss slammed into her in waves. "Merciful heavens!" She stifled her scream with a hand to her mouth. Seconds later, she slumped against the shelf with a tired but sated smile as contractions rocked her core. "You do not play fair, Major." She lifted a shaking and attempted to repin her hair.

Cornelius chuckled. "It seems you were either quite desperate for satisfaction, or you still retain the schoolgirl crush." He whipped a handkerchief from his pocket and wiped the moisture from his face.

"Cheeky. I'll never tell." She glanced pointedly at the bulge in the front of his trousers as he stood. When she reached for him, he captured her hand in his. "Shall I alleviate that for you?" What sort of woman was she to even offer? She barely knew this man, despite their history, and she'd certainly only done the same to

Weymouth twice in the whole of their marriage, hoping to stimulate him.

"Not just yet." He grinned and then tugged her into his arms and brought his lips crashing down on hers. Pulling away, he winked. Clearly, not repentant at all. "I won't apologize for that."

"I didn't ask you to."

He looked at her with speculation in his eyes. "You are surprising, Lady Weymouth, in a good way."

Residual trembles played her spine, and she shivered. What she'd allowed him to do wasn't proper, and even though she had a crush on him years ago, that didn't mean she'd carried a torch for him over the years, did it? If even a whisper of this got out, her brother would be furious.

A faint thump from the level overhead brought her back into the present. One or both of the owners were moving about. "I'm sorry, Major, but it seems I don't have what you're searching for here." Though she had no idea his taste in women—or reading material—that had to be the answer, because she wanted more from her life than an empty dalliance with a well-known rogue.

Didn't she? But yet, now that everything she'd relied on before was about to be gone, why shouldn't she pursue something that was purely scandalous and just for her?

"Ah. Too bad." Emotions she couldn't read flickered over his face in the winter sunlight. A frown tugged his sensual lips downward. "No matter. I'll leave you to your other customers."

She nodded. "That doesn't mean I won't find what you are searching for soon. Perhaps you should check back, and often."

His expression shifted, lightened, and curiosity reflected in his brandy-hued eyes. "Indeed, I might."

"Or perhaps try the rout tonight." *Oh, Penny, you are a fool.*

Surprise jumped into his eyes. "I will. Thank you." Finally, he grabbed his cane and then left the aisle.

"Dear heavens." She sagged against the shelf. Seconds later, the cheerful tinkle of the bell over the door sounded, marking his departure.

Damn your eyes, Major.

CHAPTER FIVE

No. 10
Manchester Square
Marylebone, London

A FTER DRESSING IN his requisite evening clothes, Cornelius popped down to his drawing room, and feeling restless, poured a measure of brandy into a cut-crystal glass. He needed to clear his head, but there had been no time to go for a drive despite the cold air, all because he'd promised to attend a rout tonight in the hopes of seeing Penelope.

What the hell is wrong with you, Montgomery?

Taking a large gulp of the brandy, he swallowed and relished the burn of the alcohol in his throat as he delved deeper into his thoughts. Yes, he'd dallied with women before, but he couldn't evict Penny from his mind. Yes, he'd fancied himself in love with her long ago before he'd left for the war, but that was when he'd been a different man, possibly a *better* man, and now the world had changed; *he* had changed.

And not in a good way. The war had taken much from him and had given nothing back except demons in his head and scars on his body.

As another sip burned its way down his throat, he continued to berate himself. What sort of a man brought a marquess's widow to release in a bookshop where God and everyone could have seen? And she was his best friend's sister besides? He should behave toward her like a brother, yet there was an underlying attraction, a heated desire between them that rendered all the best intentions null, as evidenced by what he'd done to her earlier today.

"What the hell, Major?" The sound of Birchfield's voice yanked Cornelius from his thoughts. "As I came up the road past your house, I noticed your carriage still at the curb and you not in it. Why do you delay?"

Well, damn.

He bit back a groan, for the last person he wanted to converse with was the earl. "How did you know I would attend the rout tonight?"

"I spoke with Penny earlier at home. Since she and I were attending the rout anyway, I said I would pick her up and escort her. She mentioned you'd dropped by the bookshop to say hello, and that she'd invited you to the rout."

Cornelius's chest tightened. At least she hadn't told her brother everything that had happened. "Is she waiting in the carriage?"

"Yes. I didn't expect to be up here long."

"She must be freezing." He downed the remainder of the brandy then set the glass on a nearby ivory-inlaid table.

The earl shrugged. "She has a heated brick for her feet and a fur-lined lap blanket. Besides, it would be improper for her to come inside a bachelor's home."

Cornelius's mind scudded off to a wicked place. Then it was all right for Penny to come inside the bookshop from his fingers and tongue? Catching a grin at the last moment and keeping it from growing, he shook his head to clear the thoughts. "My outer things are with the butler. We can leave at any time. I was only delaying because I detest the cold."

"Fair enough." Birchfield nodded. He peered closer at Cornelius. "You seem different tonight, old chap. What gives? Did you bed another beauty? Have a new woman under your protection already?"

Heat crept up the back of his neck. "Not exactly, but I *did* bring one to pleasure today."

"Oh?" Interest lay stamped on his best friend's face. "Do tell. Naïve innocent, wicked widow, bored duchess?"

Dear God.

"What difference does it make?" Though he hadn't said that lady had been Penny, it wouldn't matter all that much if the name remained a secret.

The earl headed to the door. "She's affected you differently, it seems."

"How can you tell?"

"There is a lightness to your eyes that wasn't there before. Shadows linger, of course, but you are more relaxed than you were last night."

Was that true? Difficult to say. "What should I do about it?"

"Besides bed her?" Birchfield asked as they both entered the corridor and headed toward the stairs. "Why not pursue her and see what happens?"

Cornelius frowned. "Why?"

"You deserve to be settled in your life, have all the happiness you can. It's not good for a man to go it alone, I think. Perhaps it will go a long way into helping your mental state."

"I could say the same of you." They were both quiet as they gained the floor below. "I shall give it some thought, but I rather doubt I'm looking for permanency."

And God help him if the earl discovered it was his sister at the center of this discussion. On the other hand, if Birchfield managed to kill him, at least the nightmares would cease.

⇒⇒⇒⟫⟪⇐⇐⇐

A HALF HOUR into the Fortners' rout, Cornelius couldn't imagine himself more bored than he was in that moment. It wasn't much the rout itself, but the host and hostess trying to push their twin daughters upon every man who wasn't married.

Additionally, he grew increasingly more annoyed with watching Penny speak with other men as Birchfield took her around and introduced her to them. Damned Johnathan. Why couldn't he just let his sister mingle and talk with whom she wanted? Then he wondered why it mattered to him at all. He had no right to her or her time, regardless of the scandal they'd gotten up to earlier that day.

Undoubtedly, she would be matched to someone, or at least highly encouraged to choose a few potential suitors, and by year's end, one of those men would ask for her hand. All because her family considered her unable to make her own decisions or guide her own life.

With a stifled huff, Cornelius slowly made his way out of the drawing room. Before he could make his way down the staircase, a soft hail stopped him.

"Major, wait!" Urgency in Penny's voice shivered over his skin.

He paused with his free hand on the newel post while a few guests laughed and chatted in the corridor outside the drawing room. Why did fate insist on tempting him? "What is it?" he asked as she caught him up.

The gown of gray-blue taffeta brought out the color of her eyes, but he couldn't quite keep his gaze from the low-scooped bodice beneath the thin, crocheted, ivory shawl. A butterfly-shaped broach with blue stones inside the wings winked from her upswept hair.

"Where are you going?"

"Some place that isn't here." God, now he remembered why he hated being out in society. It reminded him of everything he couldn't have and all the things he would never be. Yet he was a fool, especially where she was concerned. "Would you stroll with me in the rear gardens? I'd like to hope it won't be so damned hot down there."

"Oh, of course." Surprise lined her face. "Why?"

"Why not?" He went down the stairs, and the whisper of

skirting assured him that she followed. "Besides, I, uh, wished to talk with you after what happened earlier today." He gained the ground level and then immediately headed for the door at the rear of the house. "Also, the company in the drawing room is beyond dull."

"Agreed, on both counts, and I do adore walking in the brisk weather. Weymouth only enjoyed being outside when the weather was fair." She made a sound in her throat he took for annoyance. "But there is a special sort of magic in walking while it's raining or even snowing."

The more he learned about her deceased husband, the more he thought the man an idiot not to spend the time with her. "Do you wish to find a cloak or other garment to protect you from the winter's chill?" When she declined, he nodded and continued outside into the garden. Immediately, the night closed around him. He breathed in a deep lungful of crisp air and then let it out slowly.

"What you dared to do in the bookshop today…"

"I know, and it was not well done of me. Johnathan was right there. He could have seen, and yet I took full advantage of your inability to say anything."

She strolled through the small space with a hand on his sleeve. "That wasn't what I wanted to say." Her fingers squeezed on his arm. "The sad fact was that I hadn't been touched like that by my husband in many years before he died, so it was very much appreciated today."

That shocked him. "Damn. I had no idea, but I am glad I was able to give you that release you've waited so long for." He'd succeeded where her husband had failed. Then, feeling a bit wicked, he asked, "Would you like to walk in the square beyond? It's late enough that not many people will be able, especially with the light snow."

"I would, but why would you offer?"

He shrugged. "So you can walk, for you enjoy it." The glimpse of a budding smile that curved her mouth was well worth the effort of guiding her through the garden gate and into the square beyond. When she wasn't inclined to introduce a topic, he began. "Tell me about your marriage. You've let slip enough bits and pieces that now I'm curious. Did you enjoy being married?"

An aggrieved huff escaped her. "It was difficult the first couple of years, but then we fell into a routine. He showered me with extravagant gifts, took me on trips, yet didn't spend much time with me. That wasn't what I thought marriage would be at my age. I'd always thought something was lacking."

Did she mean by bedroom endeavors? He was too much a coward to ask. "Many women would say that was a perfect union."

"I am not those women." Again, her spirit showed, and it had arousal surging through him. "Mine was a lonely marriage on many fronts, if you want the truth. I passed the time with visiting friends or immersing myself in causes and charities. But since there was no chance of having children, I felt a bit trapped after a while, as if there were no purpose to me wedding the marquess."

He nodded. "You wanted children?"

"I did. It was an overwhelming craving and as a young woman."

Which she'd wasted on a sterile, emotionally bereft and inattentive man. "And now?"

"It would depend on the man." Her shrug only lifted on shoulder. "Being a widow of some means offers me the opportunities to do whatever I want." She glanced up at him, met his gaze in the darkness. "Weymouth's brother is in the process of moving house to London. I organized the country property for him. Once he takes possession of the townhouse, I'll need to make my own plans of where to live and how to conduct the remainder of my life."

"Ah." A bit of panic went through his chest. He couldn't lose her when he'd only just rediscovered her, assuming she wished to live outside of London. Then he shook his head. What difference did it make, truly, for she wasn't his, and she never would be.

The light snow came down, swirling about them as they strolled through the square. Rectangles of golden illumination dotted the backs of the townhouses that lined the space. There was a bit of an angelic hush in the air that allowed the soft hiss of the snowflakes hitting tree branches and the ground.

Not wanting to go back to the rout, Cornelius tugged her into a knot of trees off to one side of the square. Comprised of evergreens and oak trees, it allowed for decent cover from any prying eyes. The weather assured there wouldn't be many people about, so he took full advantage by whisking her into his arms and fitting his lips to hers. And damn the consequences. These were the kisses he should have had with her had he not taken a bloody commission with the military.

With a barely audible moan, Penny lifted onto her toes and slipped her arms about his shoulders as she pressed her body into his. Several moments went by as they explored each other's lips and mouths. Tongues met and tangled; gloved fingertips began to wander. When she pulled away, he assumed it because she was finished with the embrace, but with quite a cheeky grin, she quickly removed her kid gloves. Once she'd tucked them into her reticule, the lady surprised the hell out of him when she put a hand to his frontfalls.

"Penelope? What are you doing?"

"Giving you the same attention you did to me earlier today."

Bloody hell. "I don't think—"

"Why do I have the feeling you usually don't when it comes to women and carnal endeavors with them?" When she didn't kneel to orally pleasure him, he was confused. She chuckled. "If you think I'm going to go down on my knees in the snow and mud, ruining my gown so that everyone will know what I've been doing, you are a greater arse than I assumed."

He couldn't help a grin of his own. "Then, by all means, continue."

"You'll enjoy this just the same." Penny positioned herself behind him. When his engorged shaft sprang out into her palm, she gasped. "I'm glad you are so lovely and large. I've dreamt about what you might look like…"

"What?" Another round of shock slammed into him. "You dreamed of seeing me thusly?"

"Well, not quite like this, but in other ways. What else was I supposed to do the times when Weymouth climbed on top of me?"

Amused but curious, he remained as still as he could. If she wished to explore, he would let her, for how else would she learn or become comfortable with him… or any man? "Does that mean you are pleased with my equipage?" He was inordinately anxious to hear her reply.

"Quite." And she gave his hardened member an experimental squeeze. "Which do you prefer—fast or slow?"

"Uh, your prerogative." Merely having her fingers on his length was pushing him perilously close to the edge.

"Mmm." Tentatively, cautiously, she traced a fingertip along the side of his member. "Shall I proceed?"

The light touch paired with her tart mouth and inquisitive nature made her irresistible. "Only if you wish it." For a few seconds, in the dark and shadows with the light snow falling, there was something oddly spiritual even if the pending act was directly the opposite.

"If I'm horrid at this, I'm sorry. I have only done it once." She wrapped her hand about his stiffening length, but it was her words that made him more randy than he'd been in a while.

The press of her body against his back while she applied gentle strokes to his shaft would quickly send him to Bedlam if he wasn't careful. "You don't need to do this, Penelope."

"I want to, because in this time of my widowhood, I'll follow my own dictates." Then she held him more firmly and drew her curled fingers up and down his member.

Bloody hell. He sucked in a sharp breath, for her trembling caresses had awareness and need shivering down his spine faster than the touch of a more experienced woman. "Let me show you." Gently, so she wouldn't assume he wanted control, he settled his hand over hers, guided her in how to hold his length to maximum advantage. "Go slowly. This portion of a man's body doesn't respond well to rough handling." *Good God, how am I supposed to last in this?*

After a few minutes, a faint smile curved her lips. "It helps that you are firmer and thicker than Weymouth." Soon she was stroking his flesh as if she'd been doing it all her life. Up and down her fingers went, and at the tip, she gently twisted her wrist and flexed her fingers that had heated reaction streaking through his member.

Need tingled in his stones, but just when he suggested she stop, the cheeky woman cupped them in her other hand, squeezed them with a firm insistence that had his eyes ready to cross. A moan escaped him.

"Should I go further?"

A glance over his shoulder at her showed the sparkle in her eyes. "Only if you are enjoying this as well," he managed to say through a tight throat.

"I am." With a husky chuckle, she leaned forward. "In fact, I never knew how powerful doing this sort of thing would feel to me."

With nothing else to do, Cornelius widened his stance and reached back with one hand to grab her hip. When she continued to stroke him off, push and pull at his engorged flesh, he knew he wouldn't last far past this moment.

"I can almost hear the race of your heart," she whispered, and before he could summon a response, she added, "This is probably pedestrian to a man like you, who has taken skilled women into your bed."

"Nonsense." Concentrating on anything else beyond her ministrations proved problematic. What he truly wanted to do was turn around, slam her back against one of the wide trunks of the trees, and claim her body as he'd wanted to do on that long ago summer's night, but he wasn't in the habit of taking women against their wills. And besides, this sort of intimacy between them was far too erotic.

And still her hand moved on his shaft until nothing remained of his reality except her. He thrust his hips in time to her strokes. His cane fell to the ground with a dull thud. At one point, he put his hand over hers, guiding her, wishing to be part of the act. All too soon, frantic pressure moved through his member. His stones tingled, and urgency rode his veins.

"God, I'm going to come." His breath clouded in the air from the cold.

"Well, let's see it, then." She moved her hand faster, with more friction from root to tip while she squeezed his stones with the other hand.

The fact she was curious and apparently intended to watch sent him careening over the edge into bliss. With a half-stifled cry, Cornelius shattered, fell into a violent release, and as his length pulsed, thick ropes of ejaculate splattered on the closest tree trunk. When his body finally settled, exhaustion rolled through his limbs.

"Damn." The heat of embarrassment went through his chest, for he hadn't wanted her to see him in such a state.

She snickered and maneuvered to his side. "Can I assume you enjoyed the little interlude?"

"Very much so." As if he moved in slow motion, he stuffed his flaccid length back into his evening breeches and then did up the buttons. "For what it's worth, you weren't rubbish at that. A bit of finessing will have you much sought after if word leaks out." But he wouldn't be the one to tell the tale. That belonged exclusively to him.

"I appreciate that." Her grin could have lit the night. "It was exhilarating for me."

"Cheeky."

"Well, it was retribution, surely."

Because he could, Cornelius tugged her into an easy embrace and then brushed his lips over hers. "What is between us is madness."

"Agreed, but for the time being, I don't mind." The tinkle of her laughter as she pulled out of his arms renewed his awareness of her. "Let's continue to walk, else I might be further tempted."

For what? But he didn't have the courage to ask.

CHAPTER SIX

PENNY REMAINED SHOCKED that she'd done something so intimate and wicked to the major. And it had been interesting, as well, to watch him hit release. The expression on his face had been breathtaking and beautiful. Nothing she'd ever experienced with her husband.

Here, tucked away in their temporary escape from the world with the snow lightly falling and her breath clouding about her head, she could easily pretend her marriage hadn't happened and that she'd been with the major this whole time.

Silly girl. He is not for you, and truly, he's not the marrying kind.

Not that she wanted that anyway. Freedom was too tempting. "It's a lovely night," she said in a hushed whisper as she gave into a shiver, for without being in his arms, the cold pressed in on her.

"Agreed." Then, with a faint grin, Cornelius removed his tailcoat and then draped it over her shoulders. "Put this around yourself. I don't want you catching cold."

"Won't you suffer instead?" But she was only too glad to wrap the garment about her shoulders.

He shrugged before he retrieved his cane. "I was trained to survive tougher circumstances than this."

"Yet you are no longer in the military."

"The training is always with me."

"Ah." Penny nodded. "May I ask you a personal question?" It seemed relevant to their hidden world of the moment.

"Of course."

She heaved out a breath. "In a roundabout way, it has to do with Johnathan as well."

"Oh?"

"Earlier today at the bookshop, when he kept talking to me while you were…" She cleared her throat. "Do you believe my brother was serious when he hinted at not being here? Is he so far gone in his mind as to wish to remove himself from this mortal coil?" It was always a worry regarding Johnathan, but she couldn't do much about it while she'd been married.

"Ah, Penny, that is difficult to answer." Confliction went through is expression. "And I don't know that I should even tackle such a conversation while out in the cold."

She frowned. "Why?"

"Though I know a bit of what he's struggling with, it might not be what *I* grapple with in my mind." The major blew out a breath, and it clouded about his head. "War is destructive, not just on the men fighting in it or the property that is destroyed, but also on a man's mind. We are taught to kill arbitrability, to remove from our conscious thinking that our enemies are fellow humans. Every kill takes a piece of our minds, our souls. To say nothing of what the conditions while on the march did to our psyches and bodies."

"But would he do harm to himself because he is unable to talk about what haunts him?"

He evaded the inquiry. "The war, as well as things surrounding it, affected us differently."

"Don't play coy, Major." She rested a hand on his forearm. "That didn't answer my question, and now I'm quite worried."

"No, I don't suppose it did." He took her arm and strolled back through the square toward the townhouse. "The answer is I don't know. Birchfield is my best friend, but there are some things he's held back from me, some things I've held back from him. We might understand what we've both been through, but we can't bear to bring those things out in the light to have them mock us for our weakness in not being able to face them."

An interesting way to look at it. "Was it truly that bad?"

"Whatever you can imagine, it was worse." His muscles went taut beneath her fingertips. "I wouldn't wish such things on even my worst enemy, and no one should need to make the decisions on who lives and who dies."

Unable to comfort him as she'd like, Penny patted his arm. "I'm sorry."

He nodded. "As am I."

While they walked, silence grew between them, but it wasn't the sort filled with awkward tension. Instead, it was a companionable sort of quiet that made her feel satisfied. His scent clung to the greatcoat, and she wanted nothing more than to burrow into the crisp aroma.

As a young woman, she would have reveled in this moment, in the fact that he was solicitous toward her, that he didn't mind spending time with her. That he saw her as a woman at all instead of his best friend's little sister. But oddly, it was different than she'd imagined in a way. Time had tarnished yet hadn't fully warped those ideals. To be honest, she didn't know what she felt toward him, except she desperately wanted to know what it would feel like to be bedded by this man who held sway over women in London—eligible and not alike. Penny didn't want marriage, and she suspected he didn't either, but that didn't mean they couldn't enjoy each other for a bit of scandal.

Eventually, they arrived at the gate at the rear of the garden. "Shall I escort you back inside?"

The sound of his voice wrenched her from the thoughts. "No, thank you. Could you take me home instead?"

Concern shadowed his eyes in the darkness. "You wish to quit the rout?"

"Yes." In the event he didn't understand, she nodded.

"Is it because of what we did in the trees?"

"No, of course not. That was just another bit of insanity, and I rather enjoyed myself."

"Then why? Undoubtedly, your brother will have questions once he realizes you are gone."

"Stop." She stayed his steps with a hand to his chest. "I am not in the mood for shallow conversations, men who size me up as if I were a piece of cattle or a number in a ledger book, or the jealous looks from women competing for the same men in the room." At least it was the truth.

For long moments, he peered down at her. "What do you want instead?"

That was quite the question, for there were several answers she could tell him. "I... I want a quiet place to talk and a listening ear. Can you manage that?"

"For you? Of course." Instead of going into the garden, he led her around the side of the house to the front.

"Thank you."

While Cornelius went off to the mews, Penny sneaked into the entry hall and quietly collected her wrap and his greatcoat. They'd temporarily misplaced the major's top hat, but she told them it was fine. He'd return for it later.

Once in the carriage, she gave him his tailcoat and greatcoat, and there was a moment of sadness that she didn't have his garment to snuggle into any longer. Her shawl wasn't nearly as adequate. On the ride across Mayfair to St. James's Place, she and Cornelius sat in silence on opposite benches. Perhaps their thoughts were too heavy for the cold air outside, or like he'd said, they were of a subject that couldn't easily be shared for fear of being shown as vulnerable.

It didn't matter, for being with him in this capacity was as satisfying as anything else.

The driver rapped on the ceiling. "Arriving, Major!"

That brought Penny again out of her thoughts, and she wasn't ready to quit his company so soon. "Will you come in and take tea with me? Or even imbibe of Weymouth's spirits before his brother gets at them? I…" She cleared her throat. "I'd rather not be alone. I've grown weary of that these past two years."

Briefly, he rested a hand on her knee. Tingles shot upward to lodge between her thighs. "I'd be a fool to turn down such an invitation."

Those words made her uncommonly happy. Then the driver opened the door and put down the steps.

A half hour later, the requested tea service was brought to the drawing room and the fire tended to. She told the butler that Major Montgomery would be in residence for the next couple of hours, and since he was an old friend of the family and they wished to reminisce, she would appreciate the privacy.

The butler didn't show any reaction, but he did close the double doors. Not that she cared. Once her husband's brother arrived, she would move out of the large townhouse and finally have someplace to call her own.

With her teacup in hand, she settled into one of the low sofas with her legs stretched out in front of her and her feet propped on a small, embroidered cushion. It was strange, but she could almost feel the worry and anxiety melt from her person merely from Cornelius being there.

Perhaps she imagined it because she was bemused by being in his company and that summer day long ago overshadowing everything.

Or not.

She glanced at him from over the rim of her teacup. "When my brother spoke of Weymouth, he wasn't wrong."

"Meaning?" He frowned as he poured a half measure of brandy into his cup. "Or rather, I wasn't in Town during the course of your marriage, and Birchfield never spoke of the marquess to me through letters exchanged, but I can imagine you were lonely, from all you've told me."

"I was, and a little bit lost."

"Feel free to talk if you think it might help. I'm a better listener than a conversationalist when it comes to me being the subject matter."

"Which is odd, since you are supposedly such a rake."

"A veneer, perhaps." Shadows filled his brown eyes. "Unavoidable."

"Lies to protect ourselves. We are all guilty of it." Slowly, she nodded. After a sip of tea, she swallowed. "Weymouth was my father's friend, quite a bit older than me, of course, but my father promised I'd be treated well. Which I was. Papa offered a large dowry, but the marquess turned it down."

"The least Weymouth could have done was put it into an account for your own use."

She shrugged. Was that what the major would have done in the same position? "In his mind, he probably knew he didn't need it, and didn't think beyond that." Had he been a selfish man? Probably, most were, but in his own way, he thought he was taking care of her. "Regardless, Weymouth lavished gifts on me, took me all over England. Not only to his properties but also to the seashores, the Roman baths, to the Lake District, up into Scotland, then down to Cornwall." Long trips, mostly, but in a well-sprung coach and with plenty of books to keep her occupied, she didn't mind. "It was all lovely, of course, and I appreciated that he wished to expand my horizons."

"But not what you wanted at the time." There was an intensity to the major's expression that sent tingling awareness over her skin.

"Exactly." With nothing else to do, Penny stared into the fire. "By the time our fifth anniversary came around, I had overcome the disappointment that my marriage would never be what I'd imagined. I would never have those gentle moments of bonding or feel as if I were the single most important person in my husband's life." She rested her empty teacup on the low table in front of the sofa. "Gifts and trips don't replace time spent with me. Why couldn't he merely share an evening with me without expectation?"

"I don't know. Some men have trouble with that, especially if they aren't truly in love with their spouse." When a frown tugged at the corners of Cornelius's mouth, she couldn't look away. "Was he ever in love with you?"

"Oh, I rather doubt that. Fond, perhaps, but love?" She shook her head. "I never felt that from him."

"Ah." For long moments, the major stared into the fire. "Did you love him?"

"I felt affection for him to a point, but there were no feelings that might indicate love. We were... comfortable with each other."

"Bah. He should have been so damned deep in love with you that he showed you by spiriting you off every chance he got. At the very least, he should have said something." When he met her eyes, tears prickled behind her eyelids. "Did he ever change? Grow into something more than affection?"

"No." She shook her head and attempted to blink away her tears. "He had a mistress, not much for the carnal side but for the companionship, for he and I didn't have much in common. I didn't begrudge him the mistress, for I didn't understand what it was that he needed, and he'd already had a wife before me." For long moments, she was silent. Had she already shared too much? "But eventually, I was lonely. When he discovered I'd been writing to you in the early years of our marriage, he asked me to stop."

"Yet he kept a mistress."

"What was fair for the gander apparently wasn't fair for the goose."

"Ah. I'd wondered why the letters stopped. Birchfield didn't know either." He leaned forward in his chair, and once he set his cup and saucer on the table, he rested his forearms on his knees with his hands dangling between. That only called her attention to his powerful thighs and what his shaft had felt like in her hands. "Did you not enjoy a robust carnal life? A man with a fresh-faced, young wife should have spent a good portion of his time in bed."

"Oh." Heat raged in her cheeks. "Do you want the truth of

it?"

"Yes, for you've been telling the same up to this point, haven't you?"

She nodded. This time she danced her gaze away from him to focus again on the flames in the fireplace. "Weymouth bedded me once a month, and half those times didn't end in intercourse, for he was only able to maintain that stiffness occasionally." Surreptitiously, she wiped away a tear from her cheek. "I can count on one had the times he sent me flying in bed," she admitted, in a barely audible whisper.

"What?" Shock went through his voice. "Shit. If he couldn't maintain an erection, he could have at least pleasured you by other means."

The way Cornelius had done so in the bookshop jumped into her mind, and the heat renewed itself in her cheeks. "He didn't, for I suspect he couldn't be bothered with the effort. I wasn't the one who interested him; his mistress was."

"Damn." He cursed beneath his breath. "I'm so sorry, Penelope."

Finally, she allowed herself a reaction to his using her given name instead of the shortened version. "Why do you say my Christian name instead of Penny?"

"Why not? It's beautiful. So are you. What did Weymouth call you?"

"Penny or poppet or sometimes pet."

"As if you were a relative or worse, a child."

"Perhaps." This time, she looked at him, surprised to see annoyance in his expression. At her or at the marquess? A heavy sigh escaped her. "Then it became obvious he wasn't able to father children. I struggled with my own form of mental ghosts after that, for the dream of being a mother was gone for me. And with him, it would never be realized."

"There are only so many times I can say that I'm sorry for the life you were forced to live." Pain shadowed his eyes. "I wish I had been in England."

"To do what? Whisk me away? I was married, and Weymouth would have seen you in prison." But the imagery was appreciated. "We all have our demons, and as you said, we all need to learn how to either evict them or live with them."

"A paraphrase, certainly." When he chuckled, a tickle moved through her chest. "Why did you wish to tell me this tonight?"

Why indeed.

"I needed to tell someone, and I remembered how lovely it was that long-ago summer night when we talked in the hedge maze."

His expression turned guarded. "We were different people back then."

"Agreed, but to be honest, I like the woman I am now over the young woman I was then." Briefly, she held her bottom lip between her teeth. "Thank you for listening. My mother never believed me when I brought the subjects up with her. Instead, she blamed all the problems in my union on me. So when you came by the bookshop that first day and kissed me, I was unexpectedly linked to the past." A ball of tears lodged in her throat. Why was she such a silly goose when it came to this man? "And then with what we did today?"

"Which time?" he asked with a waggle of his eyebrows.

Heat again slapped at her cheeks. "When you sent me to near insanity while I talked with Johnathan at the bookshop." She shook her head with the ghost of a grin. "That made me think of everything I'd missed out on during the course of my marriage, and I've vowed not to let any more moments slip past."

"You are still young yet, and have a whole future ahead of you with the man of your choosing." His eyes narrowed slightly. "Why didn't you take a lover? I'm certain the marquess wouldn't have begrudged you that."

Because you weren't available?

"I can't know that. After all, he *did* ask me to stop writing to you." A snort escaped her. "I'm not the sort of woman to do that. If I fell pregnant and tried to convince Weymouth it was his?

Everyone would know I lied. That scandal would have been larger than the infidelity."

Oh, why did I tell him that? Penny, shut up!

Once more he frowned. "So you tossed away the best years of your life on a man who treated you like a porcelain doll or an object on his curio shelves?" As he spoke, he gestured with a hand to one such shelf where Weymouth had kept *objects d'art* from France.

Did he think her foolish?

The thought that he might made her heart hurt. "That's what a good daughter of the *ton* does." Tears filled her eyes. "However, I'm done doing what everyone else thinks that I *should*. I want to live for *me* now."

"Good for you." The major nodded. "I'm proud of you."

"Mr. Chandler told me this morning that he's sold the bookshop, so that he and his wife can retire to a cottage in the country."

"What?" Shock again echoed in the room. "And he didn't give you the option to continue to run it for him? He could have still enjoyed a bit of income."

"He told me I was too fancy of a lady to work in a shop. By May Day, I won't even have the shop to escape to." It left her with an emptiness in her chest, and a sense of panic about the future.

What am I going to do?

"And you feel after that, you won't have a purpose any longer, is that right?"

"Yes," she admitted in a breathless voice, as she stared at him.

"You won't marry again?"

"Not unless the man in question completely turns my world tip over tail, and thus far, I haven't met a man like that."

He snickered. "More's the pity."

She frowned. "How do you know how I'm feeling?"

The grin he shot her had the power to weaken her knees had she been standing. "It's how I felt when coming home from the war. Well, after I was released from hospital."

Penny nodded. "How did you overcome it?"

"I'm not sure that I did." As shadows once more reflected in his eyes, he turned his head to stare into the fire.

"Well, I hope that, for us both, we are successful in finding the path we need to walk, because I don't enjoy this feeling of unease and not having a place in the world." For the moment, his company was enough.

CHAPTER SEVEN

THE SOFT CHIME from the silver carriage-style clock on the mantle announced the eleven o'clock hour, and Cornelius jerked awake from his light doze.

Temporarily disoriented, he looked about the room. What the devil had happened? He glanced at the fire, that had died down significantly since they'd arrived at Penelope's St. James's Place townhouse two hours earlier. When he peered at the sofa where she had been during tea, but the sofa was empty.

"Penelope?"

With a groan, he pushed out of the wingback chair he'd fallen asleep in and stood. After grabbing his cane, he went off in search of her. Eventually, he located her in the library on the main floor. "Penelope? Is all well?" The sound of his voice was overly loud in the hushed space. The room was dark, for she hadn't lit any of the candles, but there was something cozy and inviting about the atmosphere.

"I'm not certain." She seemed so lost that protective instincts rose within him. "When I realized you were asleep, I decided to let you continue since you looked so peaceful. The lines of strain had been erased from your face. You need more of that, I'll wager."

"I'll agree with that." With measured steps, he came further into the room. "So you came down to be with your books, because books are safe, they're comforting, they never change." That was one thing he remembered about her from before she'd married. Never did she go anywhere if she couldn't carry a book.

"Yes." As she nodded, a few strands of hair escaped their pins to frame her face. "And they never disappoint me. In books, I can always find an escape when life becomes too much for me."

Though he agreed, he said, "Yet ignoring everything is no way to live."

"Neither is bedding anything in skirts." One of her eyebrows rose in challenge.

"Touché." There was something exhilarating at being routed by a woman. "We all have our ways and reasons for avoiding truths that life force us to face." He watched her, wondered if she would kick him out and so she could hide. What was it that she wanted above everything in life? Would she tell him if he asked? In the dim illumination from a sconce burning somewhere in the corridor, she was an ethereal goddess.

"Ah, Cornelius. If only we could stay the way we were before everything happened to color and shape our lives."

He frowned. "Then we wouldn't be the people we are today. I'd rather have the experiences and learn the lessons than to stay naïve."

"I suppose, though I can't help but wonder if those experiences worked to break us, where if we were still naïve, we'd never know the difference and would remain happy."

"Yet happiness after hard-won victories is even sweeter because we know what we worked for in order to achieve it." Not knowing how to interact with her when she was in such a mood, he came closer. "Perhaps we should return to the drawing room."

Penny shook her head. "Will you tell me how you were injured in the war?"

He snorted. "Which time?"

A frown tugged at the corners of her kissable mouth as she drew a fingertip along the spines of the books on one of the shelves. "I realize it was probably a time in your life you wish to forget, and I respect that. I just couldn't help but notice you don't seem to need the cane all that much. It's a bit of an accessory. Why?"

God, she was perceptive, and his respect for her rose. "You are correct. The damage to my ankle, though serious, doesn't truly prevent me from walking, but I do need the cane for support now and again. Was knocked off my damned horse by a ball to the shoulder that went through the fleshy part. It's the injury that ended my military career." He tightened his hand on the head of the walking stick. "The cane provides me with a bit of security and strength I sometimes don't believe I have without it." Would she think him too flawed?

"That's understandable." Penelope didn't look at him but continued to move her hand along the books. The flash of pale skin in the barely there light that highlighted the two silver rings on her right hand caught his attention. One rested on her forefinger and the other on her fourth finger. Of the two, he recognized the smaller one, for he'd given it to her before he'd left England for India that last night they'd had together.

Why had he not seen them before? And more to the point, why did she still wear his after all this time? Had she always done so, or had she pulled it out after he'd dropped by the bookshop that first night?

"Whenever I thought of you over the years so very far away in India, I assumed you were quite brave and incredibly noble to risk your life to fight for your country."

How often *did* she think of him during those years? He nodded. "I looked forward to your letters. Sometimes, they were the only things that kept my spirits up."

That prompted a soft smile that turned the blood in his veins molten. "I adored writing them. It helped to think that you might enjoy my little stories and a taste of home."

He did, more than she would ever know. "Weymouth made you quit?"

"Yes, well, he and my mother. She said it was scandalous to

write to a man who wasn't my husband." Finally, Penny met his gaze. The same desire and need in her eyes were what currently coursed through his veins. He caught his breath. "That was a difficult time in my life when I only had sporadic updates from my brother about you."

Damn, but he wasn't nearly good enough for her. Not then. Not now either, yet the attraction between them was still far too strong to be ignored. It fairly crackled in the air. "I'm sorry. Fighting was everywhere, and then it wasn't, but in the worst of it, I thought of you, as you looked that night in the hedge maze, and I used that image as a distraction." He cleared his throat. "Still do, truth be told."

"What?" Shock and perhaps interest flickered in her expression. "Are you disappointed in how I am now?"

"God, no. In fact, you have been a delightful surprise at every turn." Because he couldn't stand to remain parted from her, Cornelius closed the distance between then, rested his cane against the shelf, tugged her into his arms, then kissed her with a hunger that had been brewing for a long time.

Uttering a tiny sigh of surrender, Penny melted into his embrace with her arms looped about his shoulders, and as she layered her body against his, she kissed him back with a hunger that matched his. The moment he slid his hands down her back to clutch the tempting curve of her arse, all pretense of politeness vanished.

His tailcoat was the first piece of clothing to fall to the floor, quickly followed by her shawl, then his waistcoat. Between each garment, he kissed her as if it were his last night on earth. When her pink gown slid to the Aubusson carpet, he knew a moment's pause, berated himself for a fool, that he shouldn't do this, but then she yanked the shirt tails from the waist of his evening breeches, and the thought flew away.

Her stays were no match for his determination; neither was her petticoat, and as his cuffs, collar, and cravat preceded his shirt to the floor, Cornelius was nearly lost in her and he'd barely done anything other than kiss and caress her. By the time he'd laid her down on one of the low, leather sofas, his hands were shaking, which was odd because he wasn't exactly a novice at taking women to bed.

She looked up at him with round eyes, and the blue-gray was dark with desire, so any lingering hesitation disappeared. Then she lifted a hand, hooked her fingers around his nape, and drew him closer, and that unspoken attraction flared all the more.

"Dear God, how you manage to make me lose every last shred of sanity so quickly, I'll never know." Those were the last words he spoke for quite some time, for his concentration on her face and form was intense.

His hands were beneath the hem of her shift while he manipulated her pebbled nipples with his lips and tongue. The gentle skate of her fingertips along the planes of his chest and over his back was as erotic as anything anyone had ever done to him. When she arched her back and the outlines of her erect nipples were shadows beneath the thin fabric, it was all he could do not to come prematurely.

Once more, he claimed her lips, and with each meeting of those two pieces of flesh, the passion between them grew. Perhaps this was merely a search for an outlet from everything that had happened this week, but he didn't care. As his hardened length twitched at her hip and she continued to explore his chest and back with her fingertips, he gave himself over to the moment.

Perhaps if he bedded her, rid that tension from his system, he could let her return to her life and he could go about his. Yet even as he entertained that thought, he knew that taking this first step would send him tumbling down a path without anything to break that fall. And certain pain at the end, for if her brother found out what he'd been to do her—with her—over the past few days, that would be it for him.

I will worry about that later.

Then he concentrated on seducing the marchioness by dragging his lips down the side of her neck. At her collarbones, he licked the hollow between them, and when she tried to caress him, he tsked his tongue. Catching her wrists in his hands, he shoved her arms above her head as she met his gaze in the darkness.

"Claim me."

"Not yet," he said in a whisper as he palmed her breasts through the fine lawn of her shift. Those quivering globes filled his hands and made him want to thank whatever deity was listening for making her so perfect.

At least for him. If only in this moment.

"I... Oh..." Penelope scrabbled her fingers over the leather of the sofa. "Cornelius, I..." Her back arched with every pass of his fingers. Each time he rubbed them over her nipples, she shivered. Then, because he needed more, it was far too easy to relieve her of the remaining garment that hid her form from him. As she only wore stockings and garters, he reacquainted himself with every inch of her skin. When he took one of those stiff peaks into his mouth, suckled it, worried it with the tip of his tongue, she moaned. "This is wonderful." A sigh escaped her. "Weymouth never did anything like this..."

God, he wanted to dig up the marquess merely for the satisfaction of killing him for his neglect of this unique and fascinating woman. "This is only the beginning." He chuckled into her skin, and yes, it was just as silky as he'd dreamed. His hold on reality was rapidly slipping away the longer he played with her nipples, her perfect, tempting, fantastic nipples—stroking, teasing, sucking, biting.

He couldn't have enough.

At her soft cry, he quickly soothed the flesh with his tongue until she moaned and writhed beneath him, asking him to stop but urging him to continue, and he began his torture all over again.

"Let me touch you," she managed to gasp while resting a hand on his chest. "I need a distraction else I'll drown in what you're doing to me."

"Your touch will only send me over the edge sooner, and I wish to draw this out because I'm a selfish prick."

"Or a rogue?" As she spoke, she curled one hand about his nape, guided him to a nipple while she caressed her free hand up and down his arm.

A moan escaped him, for her touch inflamed him. "As if I have the capacity to be anything else." His attempt at a chuckle fell far short, for it took most of his concentration not to spend. Cornelius glided a hand slowly down her body, between her breasts, along her torso, over her abdomen to bury his fingers into her curls. "More?"

"Yes." She sucked in a breath when he eased those digits along the flesh between her thighs. "But I—" A surprised cry was poorly muffled when he uncovered that tiny bud at her center that would hopefully make her world catch fire.

"It's time you learned to fly since your husband did such a piss-poor job of it." Unable to stop, he kissed her lips while he continued to worry that little button with varying degrees of friction.

"You are going to drive me to madness!" Her hips bucked off the sofa, which caused his engorged length to pulse with urgency. She dug her fingernails into his shoulder.

"That is the point. Did he not teach you anything?"

"Clearly not, and I... Oh!" A moan escaped her. Penelope pulled slightly away, breaking the kiss, but he continued with his torment, for he wanted her to experience everything. Yes, he'd already done wicked things to her, but this felt different.

"Fall into that first release for me."

"But I can't..." Then she gasped and her body went taut when he nipped a nipple and increased friction to her button.

It was the most glorious sight as she rode out those contractions with her eyelids fluttering and her lips parted in a silent scream. "Ah, Penelope, you were made for this, I think." Heat trailed through his body as he settled more comfortably between her legs.

Dear God, the woman was gorgeous! The flush of passion spread over her chest. Her kiss-swollen lips were a dark rosy hue, which her nipples matched. Would that he had another couple of hours to completely explore her form, but he rather feared that too much stimulation would cause him to explode prematurely.

"Major, is something amiss?" The concern in her whisper went straight to his stones. The way in which she regarded him with sleepy eyes, and a half grin pushed him close to the edge.

"No, in fact it is all too right." And therein lay the trouble. He shouldn't have done even this to her, but there was no turning back.

In the dim light, anticipation warred with apprehension in her eyes as she rested her hands on his shoulders. "Finish me. Claim me, Cornelius, like you would have done all those years ago. Let me know how it feels to be needed by a man who has no issue in maintaining an erection long enough to make me fly."

Oh, God.

In that moment, they were both raw and real and on the verge of vulnerability, but he didn't care. She needed him to be something specific for her, and he wasn't about to disappoint her, for perhaps he needed the same from her as well.

"Gladly." A pox on Weymouth as well as her father for making her exist in such a marriage where there was no satisfaction on many levels. "Just let me remove my breeches."

CHAPTER EIGHT

*O*H, *DEAR HEAVENS, this is going to truly happen!*

Penny was bemused as she watched the major remove his shoes, hosiery, and then finally his evening breeches. The man was wonderfully erect, and she couldn't help but stare at his hardened shaft, but then, the rest of his form was equally pleasing, for he still had muscle definition in the sculpted planes and edges of his body. She couldn't wait to run her fingertips and tongue over the length of him.

The longcase clock in the corridor beyond struck the midnight hour, and in the back of her mind, she had the distinct feeling that she was leaving behind the woman she used to be for the woman she was now.

Leaving the sofa, she went over to him the moment he removed his breeches. "Will you allow me to play tonight?" she asked in a whisper as she drew her fingertips over his chest.

"That depends on how strong my willpower is." But Cornelius swept her into his arms with a little growl and trapped her against the hard wall of his chest and a shelf of books. "Tell me you want me, Penny. No more hints and playing. If we go forward with this, there is no going back."

"I know that, and I also know that I want you, ever since you stepped back into my life." Her pulse rushed so hard through her veins it thrummed in her ears. Unable to deny herself from touching him, she stroked a hand along his jaw. The faint prickle of blond stubble rasped against her skin. A muscle twitched beneath her fingertips. With every beat of her heart, she feared she'd shatter from need. For this one moment, she wished only to feel his lips and to have his body moving on hers. Worrying about scandal could wait; trying to puzzle out her future would benefit from a delay. In this one fleeting second, there was only her and him.

"Yet I should never have come into the bookshop that night."

"Why?"

"Because I have a feeling you and I won't be able to stop with this one meeting." He crushed his mouth to hers, claiming her lips with a strength she couldn't deny; all her senses were consumed by him. The muscled length of him pressed into her softer body while the hard edge of the bookshelf provided interesting pain-tipped pleasure to enhance everything else. His arms around her were like iron bands, his fingers fire as he played them up and down her spine. The warmth of his tongue as he tangled it against hers sent warmth between her thighs. She moaned into his mouth and burrowed closer. His clean, crisp scent wafted into her nose and left his indelible stamp upon her brain.

This was her Cornelius, the man she'd dreamed of in the dark of her bedroom when she felt most alone. He'd been the one man she could never forget from her innocent dreams as a young woman; the one man she'd always wished would come back into her life if for nothing else than to lay eyes on him one last time.

Except now, she wasn't ready or willing to give him up to fate or chance. Penny threaded her fingers through the silky hair at his nape. She stood on tiptoe in order to feel the full extent of his kiss. Her sensitive nipples rubbed against the coarse hair on his chest, and she moaned.

Seconds later, the heat of his hands seeped into her rear as he gripped her arse. His fingers feathered over her skin, and she shifted her stance, hoping he'd bedevil the button at her center again. When he drew abstract patterns over her buttocks, his fingers so close to where she wanted him to be, she wrenched away to pepper his chin with kisses. "Perhaps we should move upstairs—"

"No time." He grasped her hips and ground his pelvis into hers. "Things are already quite urgent."

Daring much, she drew a hand between their bodies and cupped his hardened shaft, fondled his stones. His breath hissed. She smiled and rubbed her hand along his length.

"I won't last if you keep on."

"That's what teasing play is for."

"Vixen." He lifted her off her feet, unmindful of her squeal, and used the shelf of books at her back to leverage her upward. When she wrapped her legs about his waist, he took one of her breasts in hand, dipped his head to lick and worry the nipple with his lips.

Penny moaned, for if he continued, she'd dissolve into a puddle at his feet, especially because his rigid length rubbed against her sensitive folds. Merely as a distraction, she wrapped a hand around his length as best she could. His hot girth filled her palm and jumped when she rubbed her thumb over its tip. What would he feel like in her body or taste like on her tongue? Hopefully soon she would discover just that. "It is lovely to be in a man's arms like this."

Amusement warred with need in his brown eyes, hardly visible in the low illumination. "I'm glad to oblige." He dropped a kiss on her mouth.

A host of shivers fell down her spine and clashed with the ones invading her insides. "I haven't been with a man for years before my husband died, so I..." Her stomach clenched from nerves. Anxiety twisted down her spine. No matter how much she desired Cornelius, or how much her body clambered to be joined with his, what if they weren't compatible...?

"Shh, don't think." He shoved into her passage without warning, and then Penny's world dissolved beneath a wave of pleasure. "Damnation, you feel so good." He pulled out only to thrust again, groaning as he held his position, fully sheathed inside her. His breath stirred the loose hair at her temple.

"Oh, goodness." There were no words she wanted to waste on how he made her feel. She grasped his shoulders and tilted her hips, wriggled them in order to take him in as far as she could. His thick, long length filled her, stretched her more than she'd ever been. Each tiny movement on his part set off a flutter of sensation through her core. She pulled him closer, wanting him to move yet hoping they could remain like this forever.

It was everything she'd dreamed of where he was concerned, and unexpectedly, a tiny piece of her heart left to become his.

"Indeed." Cornelius held her steady with his hands at her hips. His gaze softened and a mixture of awe and pleasure lined his expression. He closed his eyes and moved within her. Each penetration sent glorious sensations through her body.

With each slow, gentle thrust, Penny surrendered to him. In this one moment where her fantasies and real life collided, she discovered the reality was far better than her dreams. As he slid his hands to her arse, holding her steady, while she clutched him closer with her ankles locked at the small of his back, she never wanted this moment to end.

"This is lovely." Why was her voice so hoarse, so smoky?

He grunted, opening his eyes to meet her gaze. "I don't want our joining to be lovely." As if he wanted to make an impression, his rhythm increased as did his bid to claim her. Stronger. Harder. Faster. Each slide into her sent her closer the edge.

"Please… Send me flying." Desperation filled her voice. Penny dug her fingernails into his shoulders. "I need to feel you."

"I'm trying." Renewing his hold on the outside of her thighs, the major pumped into her. Each thrust sent intense sensation racing through her every nerve ending. Books tumbled from the shelves to tumble to the floor around them.

She encouraged him with soft sounds. Intense sensation pinwheeled through her body, but she tried to ignore the warning signs in order to prolong this coupling. "Give me all of you." For this wasn't nearly enough after so many years of longing, of dreaming.

"So needy. I had no idea. Hang on," he whispered as he wrapped his arms about her and moved her over to the leather sofa where they'd started this adventure. When he laid her down, he was quick to follow, and as he layered his body to hers, settled in the cradle of her bent knees, he said, "This is exactly what I wanted, knowing that while I fought in that damned war, it had all been worthwhile because you were here, staying safe."

"That's beautiful," she managed to say while tears welled in her eyes. Then she buried her confusion into kissing his lips, and he was all too eager to go along with that.

Seconds later, he broke the embrace. "God, this is going to go quickly. I'm nearly gone." Once more, he thrust inside her body, penetrating her with an intensity that left her gasping. The new angle must have been pleasing for him, for he groaned, and she couldn't help but agree.

How had she never been treated to such a thing before? Why hadn't Weymouth been driven to such passion each time he'd bedded her? She had no idea, but with Cornelius, she felt as though she would soon launch through the roof and go across the skies like a comet. When she needed a bit more stimulation, she pinched and plucked one of her nipples, and the added pleasure sent shivers of bliss throughout every nerve ending.

That was all it took for her to shatter. "Cornelius!" Her back arched of its own accord, her toes pointed as a wave of pleasure swelled and crashed over her, sending her flying over the edge into a world of white lights and colorful shooting stars.

As she dug her fingernails into his shoulders, the major thrust once, twice more, and he, too, found his own release. His graveled cry of her name wasn't as loud as hers had been. While his shaft pulsed, he buried his face into the crook of her neck, and ground against her, no doubt prolonging the exquisite pleasure they'd found together.

The tears that had been lurking spilled over onto her cheeks. She sniffled into his hair.

"Penelope? Did I hurt you in my enthusiasm?" Concern wove through his voice as he pulled back to find her gaze.

"No, no, of course not." Shaking her head, she laid a palm against his cheeks. "I'm crying because the release was so powerful, but also because now I know how much I was cheated out of during my marriage."

"I'm sorry. That must be a horrible realization." With a bit of effort, he rolled off her to lie on his side, and when he pulled her to him, she snuggled into him.

"It was." She wiped at the moisture on her cheeks. "Regardless, this was by far the best coupling I've ever had. I guess it's true that you are quite the rake."

Even in the darkness she could discern his frown. "That is only partially true. It's a carefully curated façade, rather."

Why would he need that, though? "Hmm." Was it true or a way of deflecting her interest?

A comfortable silence came over the room while a pleasant lethargy went through her limbs. Finally, she had to speak at least one of the thoughts that trotted around her mind.

"Cornelius?"

"Hmm?"

"If we can, might we come together like this a couple more times?" An even louder swatch of silence followed the inquiry, so she rushed to fill it. "I know this sort of relationship is not sustainable and Johnathan will have an apoplexy if he discovers our scandal, but I need you in this way; perhaps it's another bit of knowing I was cheated out of that too."

Did it make her seem too desperate or too vulnerable to admit such a thing?

"Oh." In the faint illumination from the corridor, emotions flitted over his face: shock, annoyance, resignation. "Because that's all I'm good for? A quick fuck?" he asked in a barely audible voice.

She blinked at the vulgarity, but she was also grateful he didn't try to spare her feelings. Dancing around topics put people into too much trouble. "Isn't that how you live your life? How you think of women?"

"I…" He heaved out a breath, and the warmth of it ruffled the curls on her forehead. "To be honest? I used to. In fact, I don't believe I've been a good man in far too long, but recently, I've realized that sort of thinking is wrong, and that I need something else, something deeper in my life to help turn me about."

Surprise held her captive for the space of a few heartbeats. At least he was honest. "There's no harm in it, Major. Every coupling doesn't need to end in marriage. Meeting a need is perfectly acceptable, and I'm a widow now, not an innocent."

For long moments, he clung to the silence as his hand at her hip tightened. "What is it, exactly, you are asking of me? I need you to be perfectly clear."

"That would, perhaps, make things easier." As she quickly went over the idea in her mind once more, she raked the fingers of one hand through the mat of hair on his chest. "Be my lover."

"For how long?"

"Does it matter?"

When he shrugged, it wedged them closer together on the sofa. "No, I suppose it doesn't. Why me? Why not a man who hasn't been affected by the war, or by life in general?"

"Don't be an arse any more than you can help." She stroked her fingers along his brow, combed a shock of hair away from his brow. "You and I have a history. There is an inexplicable attraction between us. We certainly haven't been proper when alone together, already. And you aren't a pompous windbag." She stared into his face. "There is good in you, Cornelius. Additionally, you give me the freedom to be me while in your company. I don't feel as if I must constantly pretend to be a woman society wants."

It seemed that the longer she was in his company, the more deeply buried truths about herself insisted on coming to the surface.

"You are a managing bit of baggage, but I appreciate your penchant for plain speaking." He heaved a sigh. "That being said, I would be delighted to be your lover."

A thrill spiraled down her spine. "Thank you." Penny couldn't help her grin. For the first time in a long while, she was… happy. Burrowing more securely in his arms, she sighed. "This is how winter should be spent, don't you think?"

"It's a good lot better than hiding in my townhouse, drinking alone." And she felt his grin against the side of her neck.

Eventually, they both stirred and began the task of dressing.

"I should go home," he said, as he laced her stays, even if she would merely go upstairs to retire. "It's far too late and I'd rather not court more scandal than we've already committed."

A giggle escaped her. "Live a bit, Major. Scandal is much more fun when one has a friend to do it with them." She bussed his cheek. "Besides, neither of us wishes to marry. There is no harm, no foul here."

"Unless you fall pregnant," he said in some consternation. "I should have withdrawn, but I was distracted by how good being inside you felt."

Heat slapped at her cheeks. "Don't borrow trouble." She shook her head, yet that was a valid concern. However, should that happen, she would have bought a cottage somewhere, perhaps away from London, and wouldn't need to combat the gossip. "Until tomorrow?"

"Yes, of course." When he came near, he caught her into a loose embrace and pressed his lips to her forehead. "Stay out of trouble until then."

"The only trouble I'm willing to court is with you." Then, gathering her shawl and her slippers, she softly told him good-night and left the room, bound for the grand staircase.

One thing was certain, her fifteen-year-old self would have been in the seventh heaven of delight to know that her fantasies concerning the major would come true later in life.

CHAPTER NINE

February 12, 1817
No. 10
Manchester Square
Marylebone, London

CORNELIUS WAS RUDELY awakened later that morning by his best friend yanking off the bedclothes and roughly shaking his shoulder.

"What the hell?" he mumbled, his voice graveled with sleep and his body still weighted by pleasant lethargy brought on by the carnal activities with Penny around midnight.

"Wake, my friend. You're sleeping the day away, and I'm hungry." After tossing the bedclothes back at him, Birchfield strode to the door. "I'll wait for you in the morning room."

"I'm not hungry," he mumbled and closed his eyes again. "Go 'way."

"I won't." Again, the earl shook his shoulder. "We need to talk."

Well, shit.

Like being hit with cold water to the face, the last vestiges of sleep fled, and Cornelius came wide awake while clutching the bedclothes to his chest. Did that mean the earl knew that he'd left the rout last night with his sister? With a sigh for the lost sleep, he struggled into a sitting position and let his legs hang over the side of the bed. This wouldn't prove good. When the door to the adjoining dressing room opened, he met his valet's gaze with a shrug.

Damn, damn, damn.

An hour later, Cornelius finally arrived in the morning room, which was a good thing. His staff wasn't used to preparing breakfast for him since he very rarely indulged in that meal, but one wouldn't know it, for it was seamless how they served the earl a decent spread.

As soon as he sat across the round table from his best friend, he nodded his thanks to the butler, who brought him a cup of rich, robust coffee. Then he narrowed his eyes at Birchfield. "Why the devil are you here? I didn't get in until late, and I quite value my sleep."

Apparently unruffled, the earl continued to slather marmalade onto a piece of dry toast. "So I assumed, but that doesn't matter, for I need to ask you a few questions about the rout."

"What about it? You were there." Despite the heat of the liquid, he took a large gulp of the coffee. It irked him that Birchfield thought to barge into his home.

"I was, but when I went to search you out midway through, you had gone."

He nodded. "So I did. What of it?" When the butler placed a plate loaded with his favorites—when he ate breakfast—he nodded his thanks and took up a fork, for his stomach gave out a loud growl. Apparently, he *was* hungry after all.

Birchfield took a large bite of his toast, chewed, and then swallowed. "Someone told me you left with a woman."

A wave of panic slammed into his chest, but it helped to make him more alert. He'd need to guard his words. "I did. You know the type of man I am. It's not untoward that I would leave an event with a woman." He took refuge in another gulp of coffee.

"While this is true, that woman wasn't your mistress." It wasn't a question.

"I no longer have a mistress. Cut her loose a couple of weeks ago. Which I did tell you about, but you must not have been listening."

"Fair enough." The earl nodded as he continued to eat through the contents on his plate. "Who was it, then? A courtesan or a new mistress?"

Heat rose up the back of Cornelius's neck. How to tackle this without revealing that he and Penny had spent the night together? He was far too tired to invoke Birchfield's wrath right now. Finally, he shook his head as he scooped up a mound of golden scrambled eggs onto his fork. "No one you need concern yourself with."

That seemed to appease his best friend, for they ate in silence for a bit. Only when Cornelius was given a second cup of coffee did he feel like conversing.

"Did you at least enjoy yourself part of last night? I didn't see you during the time I attended the rout, but I did dance a set with your sister."

A slight frown tugged at the corners of the earl's mouth. "I was in the card and billiards rooms."

"Ah. So, avoiding responsibility." He probably shouldn't have mentioned the dance, but in the event someone told him later, he wanted to be a bit truthful.

"You could say that." Birchfield nodded, but concern reflected in his eyes. "I was there primarily to monitor Penny. I don't want her to attract bounders, you see."

Did Birchfield consider him that? Cornelius chewed on another forkful of eggs. "Looked to me she was bored, which was why I offered to partner her in a reel."

"She's not much the things society holds dear. Because of that, I was informed that she left the rout early. Mama wasn't best pleased about that."

"Oh?" Cornelius worked to keep his expression neutral. "Perhaps she was fatigued." After all, they'd gotten up to more than a bit of scandal during the day that had nothing to do with what had happened after the rout. Just thinking of what they'd done together sent another wave of heat up the back of his neck.

"Perhaps. Or she merely wished to vex me by having one of her friends drive her home."

Slowly, he nodded. "Well, there are other events this week. Surely, she'll have better luck at those."

"One can only hope. I should probably keep a better eye on her and not let her slip away because she wishes to enjoy her time alone." Birchfield's frown deepened. "There are a few candidates I'd like to introduce her to as possible suitors, but the damned girl takes flight whenever I broach the subject."

As well she should. "Give her time. Just now, she is finishing the transition of waiting on Weymouth's brother. Once he arrives in London, she might be in the mindset of all things societal again." But he rather doubted that. Penny was very much her own person and quite opinionated. Besides, if she wanted the freedom to go about life without being beholden to a man, who was he to tell her nay?

"That is the hope, but my sister is stubborn."

"She is, that."

The earl narrowed his gaze. "I wouldn't put it past her to gad about with a man merely for the scandal of it because she knows it will annoy me."

Cornelius shrugged. "Let her enjoy her life just now, Birchfield. She was miserable in her marriage. Surely, she deserves to have a bit of fun."

"Penny talked to you about her union?"

Well, damn. "Bits and pieces, here and there. I mean, it's not as if we've spent copious amounts of time together for a proper conversation." He was treading near dangerous territory, and it would be far too easy to give away what, exactly, he'd done with his time in her company.

"Of course." The earl nodded. "She wasn't all that forthcoming with me regarding Weymouth, so I don't know much, but then, I now realize that match was doomed to failure from the start. She needs someone nearer her own age when next she marries."

"*If* she does."

"Yes, well, I'll try to free my schedule and spend more time with her, take her about and perform various introductions."

"Good luck in convincing her of such." Cornelius couldn't help his chuckle, and when Birchfield eyed him sharply, he merely ate in silence.

Damn it all to hell. With such scrutiny, how was he to meet with her at all?

Chandler's Books and Periodicals
Mayfair, London

As PENNY FLIPPED through one of the books she needed to shelve, she hummed a song she'd heard at the rout last night, before she'd left with the major. She'd gone to bed after their coupling in the best of moods, and when she'd awoke this morning, that feeling persisted. Yes, her muscles held the pleasant ache of use, but that only made her remember the man himself as their bodies had heaved against each other.

How could she be expected to act as if nothing had happened yesterday, when her whole world had been turned upside down and reset?

The cheerful tinkle of the tin bell over the door announced yet another customer. Already, it had been a busy afternoon, but she didn't mind, for it made the time pass quickly. Since Mr. Chandler talked to a different customer at the counter in low tones, she glanced toward the door, and when her gaze landed on Cornelius, her heart gave a queer little leap.

Oh, heavens, he is so handsome!

"Good afternoon, Major." It was unexpected, see him just now, but she didn't mind. As surreptitiously as she could, she roved her gaze over him, taking in his gray breeches, the sky-blue satin waistcoat, and the jacket of sapphire superfine. "I'm surprised to see you back. Did you need another book?" she asked, as she left the book on her cart and approached him. Not that he'd needed the first one. The way his blond hair fell over his brow made her fingers itch to comb it back, but it was the way he grinned, as if he held a delicious secret, that made her pulse quicken.

"Hullo, Lady Penelope." There was a certain twinkle in his eyes that sent flutters through her lower belly. "You were so helpful the other day, I'm hoping you can lend your unique assistance again." And since he was faced away from Mr. Chandler, he winked.

Heat went through her cheeks. "Of course. What are you in the mood for?"

"Besides you?" he asked in a barely audible voice that further provoked the warmth in her face. Then he cleared his throat. "I'm thinking a book of poetry or perhaps one of Shakespeare's sonnets."

"Both lovely choices. Come with me." A bit weak at the knees, Penny led him toward the first shelf to the section farthest away from Mr. Chandler. Since the owner was working with her today, there was no chance of scandal with the major. "We have a small section devoted to Shakespeare, so hopefully you can find something that suits your mood." At the shelf, she kept her focus on the book spines and whispered, "Why are you really here? I can't get away, because I'm closing the store tonight."

"I wanted to see you," he whispered back as he, too, pretended to peruse the stacks.

"Do you have regrets about last night?" Her hand stilled on the books. "Also, please don't ruin what we shared by getting up the nodcock idea that we should marry due to scandal."

"As if I would do either of us the disservice," he said with a grin. He shot her a mischievous glance. "I merely wished to see how you fared, to make certain you are in good health. We were a bit rambunctious last night."

The heat renewed itself in her cheeks. "I'm quite lovely, in fact. As if I have a new outlook of sorts." Just thinking about how they'd spent the night together renewed the flutters in her belly. "Knowing what I do now, I rather doubt I was living fully during my marriage." She blew out a breath. "I mean, I had my charities to keep me busy, but that…"

"Understandable." Surreptitiously, he slipped his fingers over hers on the pretense of reaching for a book. "By the by, your brother came to see me this morning. Roused me from my bed, in fact."

"What?" In her shock, Penny dropped a book. It fell to the wooden floor with a dull thud. With a quick, reassuring glance at Mr. Chandler, she stooped, retrieved the book, and put it back on the shelf. "Why?"

The major shrugged. "He's incredibly nosy, for he wished to know who I left the rout with."

She gasped, and when Mr. Chandler frowned, she gave him a smile. "What did you tell him? You didn't give up our secret, did you?"

"Of course not. That is something strictly kept between you and I." His whisper was quite thrilling, and she couldn't help but watch his lips as he spoke. "Besides, Birchfield is the worst gossip of them all; he doesn't need to know anything about what happened yesterday. Also, I didn't want him cleaning my clock if I said I was with you in a very satisfying and scandalous way."

"A few times," she couldn't help but add, with a half-stifled giggle.

"Exactly." When he grinned, her heart skipped another beat.

Penny pulled a book from the shelf. "Do we continue to sneak about?"

"Since your brother assumes I've procured a new mistress, I'd say we have no other choice unless you wish to incur his wrath."

The fact that Cornelius was in agreement they should continue to be together set off butterflies in her belly. "Not just now." She cracked open the book, but the words swam in her vision because her concentration was on the man standing next to her.

"This book might be what you're searching for. It's an anthology of a few of Shakespeare's shorter works. You can browse through to the ones you're interested in, and it will give you a broad view of some other aspects of his writing." What she wouldn't do to drag him behind that third bookshelf and shamelessly kiss him! Already, the clean, crisp scent of his cologne was about to drive her into madness.

"Thank you. This should be just what I need." When the major took it from her, their fingers brushed, and it was as if an electric charge went through her arm. He flipped through the pages, clearly on the pretense of browsing through it. Without looking at her, he whispered, "When next do you wish to meet? After yesterday, I find my passion for you won't be easily quelled with only that one meeting."

How romantic were those words? A shiver of need went down her spine. "Why not here, tonight?"

"What of the Chandlers?"

She offered a grin, for things would work splendidly. "They are having dinner at the home of one of their friends. No doubt games and cards will follow, for they are all quite close." She tidied a row of books. "They won't come back to their rooms upstairs until midnight, I'd guess. It's a standing meeting this time each month, and when they fall to talking, the hours grow quite late."

"Good idea." Cornelius closed the book with a snap. The maroon linen cover provided a contrast to his ivory kid gloves. "Perhaps we'll get up to scandal, perhaps not, but I'll come by, nevertheless. It matters not to me how we spend the time."

If she were alone, she would have danced in place. As it was, she curbed the urge to do anything untoward. "Thank you. I close the shop near six o'clock, but be warned. I will require payment in kisses, perhaps a few caresses."

He snorted. "As if I would deny you that."

Heat had returned to her cheeks. "I shall see you then."

"I'll be here." He held up the book as Mr. Chandler glanced

their way. "I'll take this one, and I appreciate your knowledge in these matters, Lady Penelope." He winked at her. "Thank you for your assistance, and since the winter nights are long, no doubt I'll go through this one all too quickly."

"Such folderol." But she couldn't help her own grin. "You are most welcome, Major, and I am a bit jealous, for you have many happy hours of reading ahead of you." She waved a hand. "If you'll go over to the counter, Mr. Chandler will take care of the transaction."

Then she turned back to the bookshelf until she could gain control over her emotions. There was something about that man she couldn't put her finger upon, but she was as giddy as a girl just out of school to have planned an assignation with him.

You are naught but a ninny.

For the moment, she didn't care. It was far too intoxicating flirting with such happiness that she wanted to horde the feeling to herself a while longer. Society and her brother's wrath be damned.

CHAPTER TEN

Later that evening

AN HOUR BEFORE he was due at the bookshop, Cornelius made certain he dressed carefully, for he wished to impress Penny beyond the skills of his carnal prowess. By the time his cravat was finally to his valet's liking, and he'd scooped up a pair of kid gloves from his bureau, a knock sounded on the door to his dressing room.

After thanking his valet, he opened the door. "I'm on my way out, Carver. Please have my carriage brought around."

"I will, of course, Major, but there is a Lady Bolton waiting in the downstair parlor for you. She says she won't go away until she has the chance to speak with you."

Well, fuck.

He never thought to see the woman again, after he told her that he'd tired of her services. She'd barely been his last mistress for more than a month. Thank goodness he'd not started the process of renting her a townhouse, and he was even more thankful he'd not given her expensive gifts. "Are you certain?"

The butler, a distinguished man in his late fifties, nodded. "Quite."

"Damn." Cornelius rubbed a hand along the side of his face. He couldn't ignore her as she would continue to call. "I might as well beard the dragon." It was the farthest thing he wished to do, but there was nothing for it.

"Very good, Major. Shall I order tea?"

He snorted. "God, no. Let's not give her any excuse to linger, shall we?"

The butler nodded, but didn't comment.

With a huff of annoyance, Cornelius followed a few minutes later. He strode into the parlor, which was at the rear of the home. This was a huge inconvenience, and he wasn't best pleased to need to confront the woman. As soon as his gaze fell on the woman—a lady only by marriage and an unhappy one at that— his chest tightened. Not in anticipation, but in annoyance.

"What are you doing here? I was quite adamant we were through when I broke off our relationship two weeks ago."

Lady Bolton frowned. The anemic winter sunlight coming in from the one window glimmered off her pale-blonde hair. "*I wasn't done, though.*"

"You have a husband. Why not use your wiles on him? Try to seduce him?" As he spoke, he crossed his arms at his chest and frowned. Though her form was quite lush and her lips full, he found those charms no longer tempted him, for her eyes were the wrong color and there were no caramel highlights in the blonde tresses.

I much prefer Penny's looks, for they aren't contrived or overblown.

"I don't like him nearly as much as I do you, and his body isn't as delicious either." She drifted closer to him with that certain look in her eyes that spelled trouble for him.

"Ha." His chuckle held no mirth. "That is not how such things work."

Of course the woman pouted. "Don't be like that, Major." Lady Bolton sidled over to him and laid a palm on his chest. Ordinarily, he would have had an immediate reaction to her touch, but oddly, there was none of that now. "I'm sorry you were cross with me before. I will do better at keeping you happy." There was a decided purr in her voice.

His frown deepened. "You should find happiness in yourself. You should also be content in that companionship, instead of what I do for you or what I can give you."

Would he ever be needed, wanted, for the flawed man that he was? Would Penny want him after she found out why he was haunted?

Lady Bolton shook her head. "I want you back. Life is so dull without you in it to provide spice and excitement."

A huff escaped him. "I'm not available."

Shock lined her face. "You replaced me already?"

Heat crept up the back of his neck. "Not in the ways you think." Did he consider Penny his new mistress? Of course not. That wouldn't be respectful, but there *was* something between them he wished to explore, and now that they'd shared intercourse, he might need to think of her as his lover.

At least until he'd gotten his fill of her. Right? He couldn't answer that from his conscience. There was something more to her; she had substance about her that many other women would never have. And that intrigued him.

"Why are you so cruel, Cornelius?" Lady Bolton pouted. "Let me show you what I can still do for you." She nipped his chin while sliding a hand down his body to rub over his length.

Ordinarily, he would have already been erect and ready, but she wasn't who he wanted in his bed any longer. That thought was shocking enough, but when he thought of her touch or her kisses, the realization that he only wanted that attention from Penny left him almost breathless. As quickly as he could, Cornelius removed the lady from his person. "I meant what I said, Cynthia. We are finished."

"You don't mean that. Don't you remember how good we were together?"

He briefly pointed his gaze to the ceiling before focusing on her again. "You're fooling yourself. Find a new protector." Not that he'd been hers for long. "Work things out with your husband."

She didn't take rejection well. "You think I'm not good enough for you." When he remained silent, anger snapped in her eyes. "You're chasing someone else, a younger, prettier version of me, a true lady, perhaps."

"That is not your concern." The conversation was over, and he wanted her evicted from his home.

A sound of annoyance left her throat. "You are not that wonderful of a prize yourself, Major. What will your new ladybird do when you try to kill her in her sleep for no other reason than you woke up disoriented beside her, and still thinking you're in the war?" The glare she rested on him could have singed lesser men. "One of these days, you'll go through with it, and then there will be trouble."

He refused to let her see how those words affected him, for they played directly into his insecurities and worries. "I'm well aware of my failings." And he'd rather take his own life over harming one hair on Penny's head.

"Well, when you're done trying to lift your position and remember who you truly are, I'll take you back. I'm not a social climber like you apparently are." Then she flounced from the room, a personification of wounded pride.

And she was a liar. She wanted nothing else but to climb through society in any way she could. What she'd wanted with him, a mere major, he had no idea. But that wasn't who he was. He didn't give two braces for society; he only wanted to spend time with Penny.

Did that mean he was on his way down the slippery slope to love?

Perish the thought…

BEFORE HE FINALLY had his driver pull up in front of the bookshop, he'd had a few errands and meetings to take. Now, as the darkness of evening crept upon them, he closed the door to the carriage then he moved forward to address his driver.

"I intend to walk home once I'm through here. There is a chance I'll have other business in Mayfair afterward." That was, if he were fortunate and Penny wished to indulge in scandal. If she didn't, then he'd need that walk to drive away lingering desire.

"Have a lovely evening, Major." The driver touched the brim of his hat before guiding the horses down the street.

As soon as he pushed open the door to the bookshop, the tin bell tinkled, and anticipation swirled through his being, for he couldn't wait to see Penny again.

"Welcome, Major!" the owner, Mr. Chandler, called out with a bright grin. "You must enjoy what we have to offer here since you're back for a third time."

That was an understatement, but it had nothing to do with the books within.

"Good evening, Mr. Chandler. I've come to browse, but I'll try to be quick." Trying not to be obvious as he glanced around the shop, he kept his disappointment to himself when he didn't immediately spy Penny.

"Good enough. We will close in a few moments, Major. Was there something wrong with the book you bought earlier?" He eyed the few parcels Cornelius brought in with him, but he didn't comment upon it. Thank goodness.

"Uh, no. It was perfectly fine, of course, but I thought I might like the volume of poetry Lady Weymouth recommended yesterday." He cleared his throat. "Is she around? I'd like to tell her goodnight."

The older man nodded. "She is upstairs with my wife helping her to dress. We have dinner with friends tonight, you see, and my wife has never employed a maid."

"Ah."

Mr. Chandler frowned. "Might I ask you a serious question, Major?"

"Of course."

"Do you hope to court my shop assistant?"

The directness of the inquiry took him by surprise. "I... I'm not certain." Is that where he wished to head? Did he want an expanded relationship with Penny over and above the carnal?

"Yet, unless I miss my guess, you've brought her a few gifts." The other man flicked his gaze to the parcels Cornelius still held.

"Yes, well…" Heat sneaked through his person. "She is my best friend's sister. Haven't seen her for a bit while I was in India with the military, and I'd acquired a few bits and bobs for her during that time." It wasn't exactly a lie, but it wasn't the full truth, either. Some of the items had come from India, but others he'd purchased for her today at the shops.

"I see." The older man looked him over as if he were assessing whether or not Cornelius was good enough for her. He suddenly hoped he found favor with this man. "In lieu of her father, I'll tell you this. Don't trifle with her affections or think to hurt her. Penny is a lovely woman who didn't deserve the marriage she was handed. In fact, she needs someone to see her for who she is, not something to have or possess."

Sage words, of course. Cornelius nodded. "I quite agree with you, and you have my promise I won't hurt her. She is far too precious to be taken advantage of, or neglected a second time."

They stared at each other for long moments before Mr. Chandler nodded.

"Good, because I won't stand for that. And if I discover you are merely using her, I will run you out of here with violence if need be."

"Understood." His chest tightened. "I appreciate that you look out for her. She needs that in her life, I think."

The other man nodded, but a muscle in his cheek ticced. "She is much the daughter I never had. Frankly, she's a special soul."

"Agreed." It spoke to her character that someone held her in such regard. "I'm glad she has you and your wife. Everyone needs supporters."

"Yes, and she'll only have us a bit longer, then I'm afraid the wife and I are off for the country. We'd like to enjoy what life we have left to us without filling it with toiling at a trade." He frowned and his eyes went misty. "Ideally, I would like to see her settled before that happens, else I'll worry about her. I wouldn't put it past her brother to offer her up to the highest bidder."

A trace of annoyance went through Cornelius's chest as he nodded. "I'm sure things will come about, Mr. Chandler, but if you're concerned, I can promise that I'll look after her, and I can assure you I won't let Birchfield send her off to a man who doesn't deserve her."

"I appreciate that."

Further conversation halted, for Penny emerged from the narrow wooden stairs with a bright smile and curiosity in her eyes. When her gaze alighted on him, her whole expression illuminated. "Good evening, Major. It's good to see you again." Then she turned to Mr. Chandler. "I hope you and your wife have a lovely time tonight. It does my heart good to know you have an active social life."

The older man grinned. His whole expression softened. "Thank you, my lady." Then he bounced his gaze to Cornelius and sent him a speaking glance. "Well, I'll just go collect dear Mrs. Chandler, shall I? I'm quite hungry this evening."

"Enjoy your evening, Mr. Chandler." Cornelius gave them space. While holding his parcels, he pretended to peruse the nearest shelf as Penny followed the man back upstairs.

Eventually, the older couple left the shop, and Mrs. Chandler sent him a look brimming with speculation as they went. He merely grinned and waited patiently until he was finally alone with the object of his desire, or rather, the woman he couldn't evict from his mind. "Well, I suppose we can now begin our evening together." Feeling cockier than he had in quite a while, he removed his top hat and rested it upon one of the shelves.

"I have looked forward to that all day." As soon as she pulled the shade on the door down and tugged the drapes across the bow window, he snaked an arm about her waist. She came into his arms as naturally as if she were always meant to be there. "So it would seem you have too."

"Perhaps." The faint floral scent of her skin wafted to his nose, and the heat of her called to him. He lowered his lips to hers and gently kissed her for no other reason than he meant what he'd said the other day: She should be kissed and often. When he loosened his hold slightly, he grinned at her. "Do you want to see what I've brought you?"

"In a bit. Right now, I'm perfectly content to be with you."

A queer little skip went through his heart, but he ignored it. Perhaps he was still unsettled after that visit from his previous mistress. After he'd divested himself of the gloves and tucked them into a pocket of his greatcoat, he grinned. "I like the sound of that." Then he took her once more into his arms and proceeded to dance with her over the shop floor.

On the heels of a laugh, she asked, "What are you about, Major?"

"Indulging you in a waltz, for I'll wager Weymouth never gave you that, and it's a damn shame, for every woman should at least feel special on a dance floor once in their life."

"How could you know Weymouth wasn't keen on dancing?" When he merely waggled his eyebrows, a faint flush went through her cheeks. The candlelight glimmered in her blue-gray eyes, and she squeezed his fingers. "Careful, Major, else people might have the wrong impression about you."

"Which would be what?" It was far too easy talking to her, as if they'd known each other in three lifetimes. Was that odd or a coincidence?

"That you're capable of charming your way into romance beyond a lark or a tryst."

"Poppycock." Romance wasn't what this was between them, was it? He was only sharing a midwinter fling with his best friend's sister.

"Are you frightened that you might be known as something other than a rake, Cornelius?" When she giggled, his world began to tilt sideways. "Such public opinion might look good on you."

"And what, let myself become domesticated? You wish me to

step foot into parson's mousetrap, set up a nursery?" Where was the panic and the disgust he usually felt when talking about such things? Hell, he'd discussed marriage with Birchfield not a handful of days ago. At that time, he was violently opposed to it. Now? It didn't sound so bad if a woman like Penny waited for him on the other side.

If she is waiting...

With each turn about the floor, awareness of her grew. Cornelius couldn't help but tug her incrementally closer whenever he could, for it felt all too right having her in his arms like this. Alone, there was no pressure to conform to society's rules, no demand to maintain a proper decorum. Her brother wasn't around to frown at them interacting like this or to toss around threats that they need to stay away from each other. There was just him and her, and this waltz with no music.

And this odd feeling of... peace.

It was something he'd not experienced since before going into the military, something he hadn't had since that long-ago summer night in the hedge maze with Penny.

Fuck.

Was that yet another sign that he had, indeed, fallen down the slope to love? Was that what it felt like, then? If so, it was much different than when he'd fancied himself in that state years ago with the woman who'd broken off their relationship in a letter while he'd in away in India. Did that mean this time would prove different?

As they slowed to a halt, Penny stared up at him with a slightly quizzical expression. "Why do you peer at me in such a way?"

"How am I looking at you?"

"Like you can't quite puzzle me out, or you've just come to a realization and are doubting it." One of her blonde-brown eyebrows rose. "Is all well with you?"

Was it? In a bit of a daze, he nodded. "I believe it is." Then, as if he were seeing her for the first time, Cornelius held her head between his palms, furrowed his fingers into her hair, and slowly brought his lips down on hers.

The kiss, not born by sexual urgency or domination, sent down roots deep into something else entirely. In that one meeting of mouths, he sought something he'd never asked of any woman before: acceptance for who he was, instead of the man he'd always portrayed himself to be. When he slipped a hand from her cheek down her back, Penny uttered a shuddering sigh and pressed herself more fully into his arms.

And for the moment, he was quite content in being utterly lost.

CHAPTER ELEVEN

DESIRE SWAMPED PENNY'S brain, and those kisses Cornelius treated her to had only served to set fire to her blood.

"Come with me," she said with soft smile as she grabbed one of his hands and led him behind the bookshelves to the farthest one where a wooden ladder was attached to the wooden frame there.

"Why, Lady Penelope, are you about to proposition me?" The teasing that threaded through his voice sent tingles of need down her spine.

"I absolutely am, but then, I suspect you have the same thing on your mind, so how much of a proposition is it, truly?" When he pulled a face, she giggled and put herself back into his waiting arms.

And they did seem quite eager to embrace her.

"This little nook is perfect for our needs, I'll wager." Then he kissed her, and she shivered with the delight of it.

"Do you mean to take me here in the bookshop?" she asked between kisses as she plucked at the knot of his cravat.

"Why not? This is as good a spot as any, don't you think?" Once more, he claimed her lips, and while he moved over her mouth, he removed the pins from her hair. They pinged faintly on the wooden floor as they fell.

"I suppose we can't very well usurp the Chandlers' bed..."

Then she completely lost her train of thought, for the major drew his lips along the side of her throat while simultaneously caressing his fingers up and down her back. Shivery sensations chased after his touch. "Mmm, this is lovely."

"And we've only just begun, Penelope." Slowly, he walked her backward until the ladder prevented further perambulation. When he pressed her against the wooden rungs, she offered no argument, merely continued to return his kisses. "Are you certain your brother won't come 'round this evening to drive you home?" The greatcoat slid off his shoulders to puddle on the floor with a dull flumping sound.

Her eyes fluttered open. When she met his gaze, the need and desire reflected in those darkened brown depths mirrored what was currently flooding her own system. "Yes. He is due on the floor of the Lords early in about an hour. I told him I'd have the Chandlers drive me home on their way out."

It was surprising and somewhat concerning how easily she'd taken to lying ever since the major had come back into her life, but if it gained her the freedom to fill her time as she pleased, it was thrice worth the possible consequences for dissembling.

"Ah, interesting. I wonder what stance he's trying to argue tonight. I'll ask him about it later."

She nodded. "If he finishes early enough, I'm to have dinner with him and Mama."

"Ah, well then, we'd best get to it, so *our* time isn't frittered away." Watching her the whole time, Cornelius encouraged her to raise her arms. "Hang on to the ladder, but don't take your hands off it."

"Why? What happens if I do?"

"Then I'll immediately stop pleasuring you," he replied with a wink, then leaned into her and kissed her again. "I don't want you distracting yourself by trying to caress me; this session is strictly for you."

Anticipation circled hungrily through her lower belly. "That sounds exciting."

"Indeed. Did Weymouth ever do anything like this?"

"No." She snorted as she wrapped her fingers around the wooden tread above her head. "The marquess's idea of exciting in the bedroom was getting fully naked instead of wearing his night shirt."

"Then all the more reason to do this now." So saying, his hands that rested on the curve of her hips slid upward to cup her breasts, and when she uttered a tiny moan, he grinned, hooked his fingers into her bodice, and with a determined tug, he brought it ever downward until her breasts were exposed and unhidden from the layers of fabric beneath. "Beautiful."

As the cool, ambient air touched her skin, Penny's nipples tightened and pebbled. "Do you plan to admire me for the remainder of our time together?" She didn't wish to seem too desperate, but the heated need that thrummed through her veins was difficult to ignore.

"Yes, but I can do two things at once." Bending, he took one of her straining tips into the warm cavern of his mouth, and her back arched, putting her more firmly into his care. With his hand, he bedeviled the other breast and nipple.

All too soon, she was inundated by waves of pleasure. When she forgot his earlier dictate and put a hand to his shoulder, Cornelius pulled slightly away, and then she understood that he'd been serious. "Rogue," she whispered as he put her hand back on the ladder, and was immediately rewarded by him rubbing the pad of his thumb over a nipple and flicking his tongue over the other. "Cornelius..." He ignored her, the rake, and continued to torment and torture her in the most splendid ways until she thought she might break apart merely from his attentions to her breasts.

"God, I have a feeling this coupling will go far too quickly," he said against her lips, as he encouraged her away from the ladder. "You've tempted me beyond my control."

"But I haven't done anything to you yet."

"That matters not. You are merely... you."

Nothing except honesty reflected in his eyes and echoed in his words. It went straight to her heart, and that organ skipped a beat. "Oh, I—" Her words were interrupted when the major whirled her about and put her front side against the wooden ladder. "What are you doing?"

"Giving you yet another new experience." When he took handfuls of her skirting and drew it up, the cool air skated over her legs and sent a shiver down her spine. Once he'd bunched the fabric at her waist, he slipped his arm about her. "Widen your legs for me and thrust out your arse."

Anticipation crashed into apprehension inside her chest. "I don't know what to do."

"Follow my prompts and do what comes naturally." His voice in her ear brought her a modicum of calm, but when he fumbled with his frontfalls and the hard length of him brushed over her arse cheek, she gave into a shiver again. "Damn, Penelope, would that we had the time so I could have you naked and, in my bed, so I could explore you as I want."

"There will be other times." At least, she hoped there would be, for she wasn't ready to give him up yet.

"God, yes." He layered his body to hers, and when she assumed he would claim her, he managed to surprise her again by snaking a hand about her hips, caressing the sensitive flesh between her thighs, and when he bedeviled the swelling button at her center out of hiding, a moan escaped her. "That's it. Give yourself over to it."

The various degrees of friction he applied to that button nearly had her launching off the bookshop ladder. When she realized he'd set a rhythm, she moved her hips in time to the movement of his hand and fingers, but since she'd already been on edge and excited from the scandal they'd already gotten up to in the past couple of days, it took no time at all for that vortex of bliss to swirl around her.

"Oh, oh…" As her body strained, Penny put a hand over his, directing him to exactly where she needed him to be. The magic of his touch, the complete trust in him that she had, all worked together to drown her beneath the sensations that bounced wildly through her. "I'm going to… Ah!" Seconds later, she shattered and was hurtled into the void while pleasure came at her from all sides.

"I'll wager Weymouth never told you how damned beautiful you are when you hit release," he whispered as he once more leaned over her, and this time he fit the tip of his member to her opening. "If he had, perhaps there would have been more connection in that union."

Before she could respond, he gripped her hips and then swiftly penetrated her passage, and didn't stop until he was fully seated.

Their moans blended together.

Penny shivered, for this coupling was so impossibly glorious. Was there any more wonderful feeling than the moment when one's body was completely filled by one's lover? And Cornelius's hard, thick length was quite lovely indeed. When he began to move, her world nearly tipped over once more.

"I won't last long," the major warned, as he renewed his grip on her hips. He dug his fingers into her skin so tightly that she feared—welcomed—what might be bruising, for then she'd carry his mark. "You feel so good."

There was no more need for words, for his actions spoke volumes. Over and over and *over* he stroked into her body like a man possessed. Each time he thrust, she pushed backward to meet him, and the new angle of penetration immediately sent her closer to the edge far more quickly than the last time they'd come together.

It was all she could do to grip one of the wooden treads on the ladder to keep herself upright as Cornelius continued to work her over. The scrape of her nipples against the wooden tread of the ladder added additional stimulation, and all too soon, she lost her hold on reality.

"I… I… Oh!" Release caught her up in its tide before she was ready, only this time, the sensation of flying was magnified, somehow, and far more intense than she'd ever known before. "Dear heavens!" Throbs of pleasure went through her, sweeping from the crown of her head to the tips of her toes, and for a few seconds, she was utterly lost to that madness.

Cornelius thrust once more, twice, and then let out a muffled shout as he followed her into that exquisite place where thoughts and sounds didn't exist. The sensation of his shaft pulsing within her brought her back from the fringes. Moments later, he collapsed against her back and wrapped his arms around her.

"Damn, Penelope. You wear me out," he said with a bit of breathlessness. "I have never been as consumed by a woman as I am with you."

She grinned as he pulled her away from the ladder. Her own breathing slowly regulated, and she turned in his arms, pressed her lips against his while residual tremors played her spine. "That was fantastic." Even she heard the awe in her voice. "I never knew intercourse could be so exciting or done in such a way." With the shake of her head, she tugged her bodice back into place as her skirts fell down. "I suspected, of course, but I feel quite the ninny being married for eleven years and not knowing…"

"It isn't your fault. Weymouth was sloppy and lazy." After he tucked his flagging member inside his breeches, he did up the buttons. "And hell, Penny, you deserved his love."

Tears unexpectedly welled into her eyes. She blinked them away while he retrieved his greatcoat and then spread it on the floor near the ladder. "That was never going to happen between us, though. There was more wrong than merely the age difference."

"And yet you were willing to sacrifice your happiness for the sake of the marriage."

"That is what one does," she managed to whisper.

"No." He shook his head. Then, taking her hand, the major tugged her down onto the greatcoat with him. "A union should take into account both parties' happiness and contentment, which requires attention from the pair." After propping his back against the bookshelf, he encouraged her to lie down with her head resting on his belly.

"So says the man who has never been married." But his words evoked an image of something she desperately longed for. A union with both people working toward a common goal with love that bound them.

Would she ever have that in her life?

"One doesn't need to have been married to know that one needs to treat their significant other with respect, decency, and love, at the very least and affection and attraction that has room to grow."

"Are you a secret romantic, then?"

He snorted with amusement. "I wouldn't say that, but don't mention this conversation to your brother. I'd never hear the end of it."

Slowly, Penny nodded as a pleasant wave of exhausted satisfaction came over her. "Tell about one of your times in the military. Did you miss home? Were you cognizant of the fact you were in a different country, or did you stick around a fort most of the time?"

"I admire how curious you are, Penelope." As he spoke, he finger-combed her hair. "Yes, there were many months wherein my work took place in and around the fort in Bombay. However, there were always clashes between the Indians native to the area and the British occupation. The East India Company had quite the swelled head around that time, thought they were superior to others, which exacerbated the situation."

"Did you see fighting?" Hearing about this part of his life was fascinating.

"Indeed. Many of the battles didn't last long, the British occupation was strong, and one thing the British military is known for is organization. That kept rebellions to a minimum. At least in that part of India. By the time I was injured and my commission expired, I was more than ready to come home." He met her gaze in the gloom, for the illumination from the candlelight didn't reach into their cozy corner. "Yes, I missed England and London, or at least a couple of things about it."

"Your mother?"

His chuckle released a horde of butterflies in her belly. "Not quite, though I'm glad she didn't do something irresponsible in my absence."

She clasped her hands at her waist. The sensation of him combing his fingers through her hair was quite lovely and relaxing. "Did you take a lover during that time?"

"I'd rather not say."

A snort escaped her. "I won't be offended or even scandalized. Remember, I was trapped with Weymouth the whole time you were away."

"True." A huff left his throat. "My time in Bombay was long, and there were times when I couldn't bear to go back because too many things had changed." He was silent for so long, she wondered if he would continue the conversation. "Yes, I had a few lovers. Two were Englishwomen attached to various officials or peers at the fort, and one was the daughter of an English general and his Indian wife."

"How exciting." She met his gaze again. "I'm glad you have always been scandalous."

He frowned. "You are." It wasn't a question.

"Yes." She nodded. "Men who constantly toe the line and follow the rules are dreadfully dull." And sharing scandal with him now continued to surprise her. When she'd been a young, innocent just out of the schoolroom, she would have sacrificed much for the chance to share such intimacies with him, for at the time, her only future was Weymouth.

But now he was gone.

"To be honest, I tend to believe I'm too far gone to be a good man anymore."

"Why? Because of what you had to do during the war?"

"That, as well as other things."

Hearing a tone of despair in his voice, Penny righted herself and sat with her back against the bookshelf next to him. "Will you let me catalogue some of your scars?"

"Not tonight. I'd rather talk to you and pretend I was someone else."

She glanced at him, caught the frown tugging at his lips, and then took his hand in hers, threading their fingers together. "You refer to what's not right in your head."

"I do." He nodded. "I suffer from nightmares, Penelope. In fact, I don't remember the last time I had a full night's sleep. The things I saw during my military career, the things I was forced to do, the sounds from men dying or in agony…" With the shake of his head, he clutched at her hand. "There are times when I wake in a dead sweat, thinking myself back on those battlefields."

"I'm so sorry." Was that what her brother suffered from as well?

"It's not just that. India, while a glorious country, is a land of contrasts. There are very rich individuals and also extreme poverty all in the same area. The way they treat each other by a caste system is cutting and devious, at times."

"Like class differences in England." She shrugged. "People always need some form of barrier to keep those they deem lower than them away."

"Once, during the night when I was with a mistress, I almost killed the woman by waking prematurely and thinking her an enemy bent on attacking me." Emotion graveled his voice. "I didn't mean to; it was pure instinct, but our relationship broke after that. Probably as it should have. That is one reason I've not cared too deeply about another woman." When he met her gaze, his was dark and tormented. "I'm too dangerous. Too broken."

"No." She shook her head. "That wasn't your fault."

"It was. I should be able to control my impulses, especially three years after I left the damned war."

Penny huffed. "Stop. You need to find other ways to cope with those problems."

"I've tried." Yet he hung onto her hand with a hard grip that hurt a bit, but she didn't wish to sour the moment.

Gently, she eased her fingers from his. "Bedding women isn't the answer."

"Agreed, but it's a distraction."

"It doesn't help."

He waggled his eyebrows. "Depends on the woman."

"Oh." She sucked in a breath. Did he mean her? "If you need someone to talk with, please feel free to call. I want to help you."

"I appreciate that. Being here with you now helps."

They sat in silence, and she considered it a bonding moment.

Eventually, Penny stirred. "You should marry, Cornelius. At least then you'll have someone looking after you. I worry over you and what will become of you." She eyed him. "In fact, I've always worried about you."

Surprise flickered over his face. "What if I hurt the next woman in my life?"

"You won't."

"Why do you think so?"

She laid a hand on his thigh. His muscles tightened beneath her fingertips. "You won't let yourself, because a man like you will only marry for love or not at all. Because when it comes down to brass tacks, you are a brave and honorable man."

"I don't know about that." Turning halfway to her, he added, "If I were all that honorable, I wouldn't be doing unspeakable things to my best friend's sister, the woman I promised him I wouldn't go near."

Before she could respond, he cupped her cheek and gently pressed his lips to hers. The tender overture had tears welling again in her eyes, and as she pulled away to peer into his face, a shuddering sigh left her throat. "Are you going to show me what is in those parcels you brought over tonight?"

"In time. Right now, I want to stay here in the silence and the gathering darkness. With you, and pretend..."

She frowned. "Pretend what?"

"That things were different." Unfortunately, he didn't elaborate, and she didn't ask for fear of what he would say.

"I'll be here for as long as you need," she said in a barely audible whisper as she rested her head against his shoulder. When his arm went about her waist, she smiled.

For the moment, this was enough. It wasn't marriage and it wasn't being married; it just... was, and she was content with that.

CHAPTER TWELVE

WHEN CORNELIUS TUGGED the pocket watch from his waistcoat and checked the time, he was astonished to see it was nearly seven-thirty. The last ninety minutes had gone by in a blur, and what was more, he didn't wish for this little bubble from the real world to fade.

As he turned his head, he pressed his lips to the top of Penny's head. Oddly, he feared he liked her more than was good for him, and that could only spell disaster for them both. Then he frowned. *Why am I so stupid?* He'd neglected to withdraw the last two times he'd come together intimately with her, and what if a pregnancy resulted from one of those couplings? He would become a father, but he didn't want to force her into a marriage out of obligation; she wouldn't wish for that either, and yet, if he didn't marry her should such a complication come due, she would be tossed from society with a ruined reputation.

Not to mention that Birchfield would drag him to an illegal dueling field and then put a ball through his heart for defiling and ruining his sister.

He shouldn't chase anything in the event it might not happen, for that sort of rejection might further poke at the demons in his brain. Stirring, he urged her head off his shoulder. "I should go. Shall I drive you home? Someone will start to look for you soon."

The look of drowsy satisfaction on her face went straight to his stones. "Of course you can drive me, but not to Weymouth's St. James townhouse. To my brother's home. Remember, I'm scheduled to eat dinner with him and Mama tonight." When she gained her feet, she brushed off dust and lint that clung to her skirts. "And I need time to change." She shrugged. "I sent a gown and accessories ahead this morning."

"Clever." He accepted the hand she offered to help him off the floor. A groan escaped as his muscles protested. "God, I feel ancient at times."

"Hardly that, Cornelius. You are still quite vital from what I've experienced."

Heat climbed up the back of his neck. While he retrieved his greatcoat, he said, "You are quite brave."

"Why is that?"

"Having dinner with your brother and mother? When they are both actively trying to match you with someone?" He shoved his arms into the sleeves of the garment.

"They mean well. And yes, their efforts—pushing—are quite annoying, but they are relatively harmless." A smile curved her lips. "But at the end of the day, I am adamant that I don't wish to marry again. At least, not right now."

Well, there was his confirmation. He nodded. "And neither should you until you're ready and you find a man you can picture sharing a life with. A life full of lovely memories and times you can both cherish."

Would he ever have that for himself?

As they emerged from the stacks, Penny shot him a look of concern. "Why don't you join us for dinner? Even a rogue must eat."

"In that case, I'd be delighted to join you." Truth be told, he wasn't enjoying the fact he had to sneak about in order to be with her. She deserved more than that. Hell, she deserved the world at her feet and a man who would dote on her for the rest of her life. Did he have the wherewithal to be that man? As broken as he currently was?

There was no easy answer just now.

After Penny donned her reticule and bonnet, she gathered up the few bags and boxes he'd left on the counter for her. "Are you going to tell me what little gifts you've brought me?"

"No." Cornelius shook his head. "I want you to have the thrill of the surprise. Open them later tonight after dinner." Would she like the fripperies he'd chosen for no other reason than he thought she might enjoy them?

"How sweet." She handed him the parcels so she could grab her reticule. "We should take our leave. My brother is a tad ornery if his dinner is delayed."

He followed her out of the shop and waited patiently as she locked the door. "Birchfield can wait. It'll be good for him." Once she finished, he led the way toward a cab stand, for it would have taken far too long to send a boy to his home in order to summon his carriage. Besides, the distance between the bookshop and his best friend's home wasn't far.

"It's so beautiful out here tonight," Penny said with a fair amount of awe in her voice as the light snow fell around them. "Don't you think?"

"I do, indeed." But his gaze was fixed on her instead.

When she caught him, the grin she shot him set fire to his insides. "Oh, you."

"You know I'll be severely underdressed for dinner, which means your mother will eye me askance."

"Mama can overlook it this once, or perhaps Johnathan can lend you a tailcoat. He's slightly broader in the chest than you, but it could work."

"Bah." He shook his head. "I'll wager I'll survive."

However, she'd been correct. The night was very near perfect. If anyone could make him want to be leg shackled, it was her, but could he trust that she wouldn't give up on him? The last woman he'd let his heart become involved with had declared him not a whole man, and she'd done it in letter form while he'd still been in India. Penny wouldn't prove as cruel, but would she consider him worthy?

Besides, she didn't wish to marry again. She'd already said as much.

Wilmington House
No. 23 Hanover Place
Mayfair, London

NO SOONER HAD they arrived at Birchfield's townhouse than the earl joined him in the drawing room while Penny and her mother went to dress for dinner.

"How lovely to see you again, my friend," the earl said, with a grin. "When Penny mentioned you'd stay for dinner, I was perplexed, for I didn't know you'd come in together. She said you'd hired a cab to convey her home?"

"It is." Cornelius made his way to the sideboard, where he poured a measure of brandy into a cut crystal glass. "Uh, I was walking through Mayfair as I do many evenings. When I came to the bookshop, I saw her out locking up. Thought I'd save you the trip of coming by."

"You're a good man," Birchfield said, as he approached Cornelius. "I'm glad you thought to look after her."

He didn't especially feel like a good man, especially since he'd put the earl's sister through her paces not two hours earlier, on a bookshop ladder no less. "I appreciate the fact that you think so." After taking a sip of the brandy, he continued. "You could have said I was a bounder."

"Is there a reason for me to think that?" One of the earl's eyebrows rose in question.

"God, let's hope not." Cornelius moved to a chair then fell into it and rested his cane nearby. "It's been a long day, my friend." But he wouldn't change it for anything.

"Why? You seem almost happy tonight, and that is most uncommonly not you. Care to explain?" Birchfield took a chair near Cornelius. "It's not like you. In fact, I can't remember the last time I saw you so… relaxed."

"Who can say?" He shrugged and concentrated his gaze on the drink in his hand. "Perhaps the monkeys and parrots in my brain have settled for a time. I really couldn't say what has precipitated the change." When he pressed his lips together, he knew, but he'd be a dead man to say. "I've recently been talking to someone, and that has helped." It wasn't a lie.

"Good for you." Birchfield's expression lit while he sipped his own brandy. "Did Penny confide in you on the ride over? She had so many parcels, I'll wager she had a bit of a shop earlier, and that usually makes her happy. I figured she might feel chatty as well."

Heat made itself known on the back of his neck, for those parcels were his gifts to her. "She did not. Was she supposed to talk with me about something?"

"I couldn't say. She's just been uncommonly… congenial, perky, really, it you will. Of course, she still has a smart mouth, but there's nothing for that."

Cornelius couldn't help his chuckle. "Well, she *does* have spirit." If it was any other woman they spoke of, he would tell the earl that she just needed creative carnal endeavors to keep that mouth busy, but he stopped himself at the last moment, for this wasn't some doxy. It was Birchfield's sister and Cornelius's lover, yet she was more than that, wasn't she?

"Well, I only asked because there is a man I'm going to introduce her to at the Valentine's rout. He's of an age with her, a determined banker, and he's the sort of man she might fall for."

"What?" His gut hurt as if he'd received a punch. "Who is it?" Even though he'd known his friend intended to match Penny, he hadn't expected it so soon nor would it ache so much.

"Viscount Middleton."

"Fuck me." Cornelius choked on the swallow of brandy he'd just taken. "That man's a rogue with a reputation."

"So says the man with an even worse reputation," Birchfield said, with a laugh and amusement dancing in his eyes. "However, Middleton has the potential not to be, if matched with the right woman."

And he wanted to dangle his sister in front of the bounder as incentive? "It's not your sister's responsibility to raise a man or change him in the hopes he'll better himself." Would the viscount be the man to turn Penny's head? The thought had the power to send him back into the doldrums. "And hasn't she already suffered enough by being forced into a relationship she wasn't enthusiastic about?"

This time, Birchfield frowned. "Well, it all depends on her, but Penny's the sort to need a project."

Cornelius snorted. "If she's not impressed, he won't have a chance. She's not a meek and mild miss any longer. She'll shred him alive." Oddly, he wanted to see that in person.

"I don't know about that." The earl darted his gaze away. "He's already asked for her hand. I'm tempted to agree, merely so I'll know she'll be looked after, and I won't need to worry."

He glanced sharply at the earl. "Are you truly planning to step off this mortal coil?" What must the other man be grappling with to even contemplate such an action?

"I don't know." The earl's expression sobered. Shadows haunted his eyes. "I'm struggling just now, especially since you have been unavailable to talk with or at least joke with and take my mind off my thoughts these past few days."

Damn.

"I've been busy." Surely Birchfield didn't mean to lay the blame on him?

"With your new courtesan?" One of his blond eyebrows rose in question.

"I'm not ready to talk about it." And he meant that. It was too dangerous to inadvertently divulge the truth. Afterward, he drained the contents of his glass in one swallow, coughing slightly when the liquor burned his throat.

"Look, Cornelius, my life right now is complicated. You more than anyone know this. Mama is driving me mad with her orders and demands. I fear that Penny will do something rash if she's not tamed, and if one more thing goes wrong, I don't know what I'll do."

Why the hell would he want Penny tamed? She was very nearly perfect as she was? But then he concentrated on his friend's words. "What happened in the Lords tonight?"

"God, it's a coil." Birchfield blew out a breath. "The stodgy old men aren't willing to agree to new ways of governing. They're afraid their lives of luxury might evaporate if we make the lives of the other people in England better. I honesty despair of the future of this country."

"I'm sorry, Birchfield. It must prove frustrating to face that each day."

"It is." He nodded. "It wears on me."

"Keep the faith." Cornelius set his empty glass on a small, ivory-inlaid table. "Promise me that you wait to ruin Penny's life until after Valentine's Day. Every woman deserves that one night to have the world at her feet and hope in her heart."

"What the hell is wrong with you?" the earl asked with a frown. "This behavior is exceedingly odd for you."

"What do you mean? I'm still the same man as I've always been." Hopefully, his expression or eyes didn't give too much away of what he'd gotten up to these past few days.

"Caring about anyone beyond yourself."

Cornelius shrugged. As casually as he could, he rested an ankle on a knee. "I care what happens to you. Should I not?"

"Ha." Birchfield shook his head. "That's a given, but why the interest in my sister?"

"Just looking after her as you would."

"Mmm." While the earl sipped his brandy, he eyed him with speculation.

Resisting the urge to tug at the knot of his cravat, Cornelius cleared his throat. "Don't you want Penny to be happy?"

"Well yes, but—"

"Then let her choose the life she wants for herself." He shrugged. "It's not that difficult a concept."

"If I do that, she's liable to open her own bookshop and live as a widow and alone for the rest of her life."

"There is nothing wrong with that if she's content." It would certainly suit her. Would she still wish to see him, or would their affair eventually run its course? "For once, let her have her head. I fear her marriage to Weymouth took much from her like the war did us."

The earl frowned. "Nonsense. Her marriage was decent enough."

"So you say, but have you truly talked to her about it?"

Birchfield's glance was as sharp as a hawk's. "Have you?"

Well, damn. He was in danger of saying too much. "Not as much as you'd like to think." Or as much as he would share with the earl.

Then Penny and the dowager countess came into the drawing room. Both he and Birchfield shot to their feet, and when his gaze met Penny's, his world tilted, for she was a vision.

The gown of a mauve-colored velvet clung to her curves as if the fabric were caressing her with a lover's touch. Her blonde-brown hair had been brushed and fashioned into a quick upswept style to hide the fact she'd been involved in a tryst not two hours before, but it was the easy smile that curved her nearly full lips that held his fascination. Well, that and the way she carried herself, as if she knew a delicious secret and had only shared it with one other person—him. The glow in her blue-gray eyes attested to the fact that she was quite satisfied with her life currently.

"You are truly exquisite tonight, Lady Penelope. It's a wonder that leagues of men haven't beaten down your brother's door to ask for your hand."

"Oh, how sweet of you, Major." A blush pinkened her cheeks as she joined him and Birchfield at the grouping of furniture.

Then the earl destroyed his honesty by saying, "That is how Montgomery is able to charm so many women into his bed. He flirts and compliments them out of hand until they're overwhelmed and flattered. No wonder they practically fall at his feet."

Slowly, Penny's smile faded. Confusion clouded her beautiful eyes. "Oh. You're probably right, Johnathan. The major is a rogue."

Immediate, hot anger filled his chest as he tossed an annoyed glance at his best friend. "In this case, every word is true. Your sister *is* beautiful, both inside and out." Then he gave his full attention to her, closing the distance and scooping up one of her hands. "I'm now thinking I should have taken my leave instead of giving it to other men because seeing you, even if you were married, would have given me strength." Then he raised her gloved hand to his lips and placed a kiss on the back.

The dowager tittered. "Well, he *is* charming."

"That he is," Penny murmured, and when her smile returned, Cornelius's world tilted sideways again. "Regardless, I'm glad you are back in circulation, Major."

"Indeed," Birchfield said. While he took another sip of his brandy, he watched Cornelius with a narrow-eyed gaze.

"Major, perhaps you could escort me to the winter carnival at Vauxhall Gardens next week." Penny moved closer to her mother. "I've been wanted to go, and Johnathan refuses to take me and Mama. Says it's naught but a way to tumble into scandal."

"Does he, now?" If the prick wouldn't do that one little thing for his sister, then Cornelius would gladly volunteer. "I would be delighted to escort you and Lady Birchfield to the winter carnival. I will also be honored to take you both to one of the evening shows if you wish."

That caught the dowager's attention. "Why, I haven't been to the opera in years. My son doesn't enjoy such things."

"All the more reason to go now," he said with a wink, then threw what he hoped was a speaking glance at his best friend.

"What a lovely gentleman you are, Major," the dowager gushed. "I gladly accept the invitation for both myself and my daughter."

Penny beamed. "It truly is a wonderful suggestion. Thank you, Cornelius."

"You are quite welcome."

During the exchange, the earl bounced his gaze between him and his sister. Did he know or suspect what they'd done together? And if so, what would happen?

For the time being, Birchfield merely nodded. "Yes, thank you for doing this for my family. I know the ladies will have a lovely time, and be well protected besides."

"Of course they will be." Cornelius couldn't help his smirk. It didn't matter that he wished to charm both Penny and the dowager. In the end, he wanted Penny's happiness over everything else, and if he could play a small part in that, so be it.

Chapter Thirteen

February 14, 1817
Valentine's Day
Needham House
St. James's Place

Penny closed the lid on the last trunk of personal possessions—this one having to do with *objects d'art* and various bric-a-brac Weymouth had gifted her over the years—with a sigh. Most everything that belonged to her had finally been packed away, with the exception of her clothing and all the fripperies she would still require until her brother-in-law arrived in London.

Though the man was due by the end of the month, it was her plan to move into her brother's townhouse until other arrangements could be made. Her husband might have been many things, but he'd left her a decent settlement, and that, combined with selling a few of the many parures he'd given her over the years, could buy her a modest townhouse. Perhaps not in a popular section of Mayfair, but then, all she wanted was a quiet neighborhood where she could silently step out of society and hopefully be forgotten.

Only then could she begin to puzzle out how to achieve some of the dreams she'd carried in her head for far too long.

When she left the downstairs parlor, she went up to the second level, for she'd accidentally left her shawl in the drawing room. Along the way, she met the housekeeper, Mrs. Potter. Her black bombazine skirting swished with her every movement and the lace on her mobcap served as a pretty decoration for her round, red cheeks and her bright, cheerful brown eyes. She'd been with Penny throughout the entirety of her marriage to Weymouth, and during that time, she'd served as a second mother.

"Good afternoon, my lady. Would you enjoy an early tea?"

"Oh, not just yet. I've been busy packing up the last of my things."

The housekeeper nodded. "I'll have Mr. Wilston put the trunks with the rest of them. Can I assume you will remove to your brother's home soon?"

"I believe so. It's not what I wish to do, but I find I can't linger here. Something about it doesn't feel right, as if this isn't my home. It was merely where I stayed when Weymouth was in Town." That was the best way she could explain it. To her way of thinking, a home was somewhere filled with love and happiness, a sense of belonging, a space where she felt safe and secure with the ones she liked most beneath the same roof. "I'm anxious to make a home for myself sometime soon."

"I will miss you, of course, but I understand. The staff are ready to welcome the new marquess whenever he arrives."

Penny's chin wobbled. "I appreciate that, Mrs. Potter. You have been a lovely friend to me over the years, especially when I was so very lonely and lost." She moved into the drawing room, for there was a decided chill in the air, and it was snowing outside.

"You remind me, at times, of my own daughters back in Hertfordshire. They have both been married for some years and have families of their own, but there are times when they still need advice from their mother." The housekeeper followed her into the room. "Oh dear, the fire needs tending to." When she reached for the bellpull, Penny shook her head.

"Don't worry about it." She slipped the shawl onto her shoulders. "Soon enough I'll begin the process of bathing and then dressing for the rout tonight, so I won't be in this room."

Mrs. Potter nodded. "Would you like the fire in your rooms lit, then?"

"Yes, please. I detest having a bath in a cold room. Even if I'll take it in a couple of hours, I'll probably curl up in my bed and read for a bit. It helps to relax me before having to be out in society." She rubbed her hands up and down her arms as the housekeeper waited on a maid to response to the summons. Once the maid arrived and received the orders regarding the fire and left, Penny pressed her lips together. "Might I have a private word with you, Mrs. Potter?"

"Of course, my lady." Concern filled the older woman's eyes. "Is all well?"

"I think so. My mother is taking tea with a friend this afternoon, and my brother has a meeting with his solicitor, so I have a bit of free time." She blew out a breath, for she didn't know how to begin, but ever since the major had come back into her life, everything had been topsy turvy. "How long have you been married to Mr. Potter?"

"Nearly twenty-five years. That's a bit over half my life."

"That is quite impressive." Penny fiddled with the fringe of her ivory shawl. "How did you know you were in love when you decided to marry your husband?"

"Oh, my dear, you just know deep down in your soul." The housekeeper's eyes sparkled as she regarded Penny. "He's so respectful and courteous, doesn't demand things from me, is a good provider and protector."

"How lovely."

Mrs. Potter nodded. "People said we were wrong for each other, but we didn't care. When you are in love, nothing else matters except that other person."

Slowly, Penny nodded. "And you feel as though you might burst if you're not with them all the time?"

"Oh, yes, dear." The housekeeper smiled. "You want to know everything about them, help them with their struggles as they'll do with yours. You yearn to understand why they think as they do."

"That's exactly it." Is that what she felt for Cornelius?

Mrs. Potter eyed her with interest. "But bear in mind, marriage is more than just the good times, the easy times. It's truly the sickness and sadness, the angry words and misunderstandings that bring a foundation to a union, and the overcoming of such to start again in a better, stronger place."

"I never had that in my marriage with Weymouth. He refused to discuss most things with me, thought that if he brought me gifts, all was well."

"Perhaps he was fatigued from his first union, or perhaps he just wasn't a man for marriage."

"True, but he should have made an effort, regardless." Penny nodded. "I'm sure your union is lovely. I'm glad for you both."

For the space of a few heartbeats, Mrs. Potter looked at her with a slight smile. "My dear, do you have feelings for a certain major?"

Penny gasped. "How could you know anything about Major Montgomery?" He'd only driven her home once, and at that time, he hadn't come in.

The housekeeper shrugged. "His name has come up in conversation." One of her eyebrows went up. "Is he special to you?"

"Is it that obvious?" Was he special, though? She enjoyed being in his company, and she liked talking with him. Of course, in this new lover capacity, it was thrilling, but was there anything else between them beyond that?

"Not to many people, but I've known you for all the years you were married to the marquess. You light up when the major is near, and I've seen the looks exchanged between you two." She winked. "That means something."

"I don't know about that." Yet the hope in her heart expanded. "My brother has already forbidden a match between us, and I rather doubt the major is the marrying kind." Was she content with what they shared right now? Would she always be thusly?

And what would happen if those two couplings resulted in a babe? For a few seconds, her spirit was buoyed with the possibility of being a mother after all this time. However, she didn't want him to offer for her out of obligation alone. That was no way to start a life together.

"Don't be so quick to discount love, my lady. It has a way of making a path where there once was none. And if there are noses out of joint, they will heal."

That was encouraging. "Oh, but I don't love the major. He is just… there."

Mrs. Potter chuckled. "Dearie, at some point, you'll need to be honest with yourself. There is no shame in who you love."

Before Penny could respond, the butler came to the door.

"Major Montgomery is here to see you, my lady."

"What?" Her heart leapt.

He nodded. "I've put him into the downstairs parlor."

"Thank you, Wilton. I'll go down directly." Heat slapped at her cheeks.

Once the butler left, Mrs. Potter smiled. "Not in love with him, hmm?"

With a smile, Penny shrugged. "I don't know, but I am enjoying what we have just now. There is time enough to work everything out later."

The housekeeper nodded. "Ring when you want your bath."

"I will. Thank you." Then she left the drawing room and tried not to run down the stairs. As she came into the parlor, her heartbeat accelerated the second she saw Cornelius. Was there any more handsome a man? "Major, what are you doing here?"

When he turned about from studying the contents of a curio cabinet full of items Weymouth owned before he'd married her, her gaze fell onto the large bouquet of hothouse flowers he held. Wrapped in delicate pink tissue paper, the pale color set off the glory of the roses and lilies nestled within, all in glorious shades of red, pink, and white.

The grin he flashed sent frissons of need down her spine. "I wanted to bring you these." When he gave her the bouquet, their fingers brushed. Trembles tumbled through her insides.

"They are lovely, of course, and I adore hothouse flowers, but *why* did you bring them?" Then she brought the blooms to her nose. Immediately, the floral scent enveloped her.

"No doubt you'll receive many gifts from men tonight as they vie for your notice, but I wanted to give you mine first, because I know the flowers you like."

She peered into the bouquet, and at the heart of the flowers was a spray of lilies of the valley. Long ago, she'd told him they were her favorite flower. Her heart squeezed. "You remembered about the lilies."

"I did, and it was the devil's own task in finding a florist who had them, but I persevered." Then he drew a small, flat, square box from a pocket of his greatcoat. "There is also this." Gently, he took the flowers from her and gave her the box.

"It's too much already." Especially since he wasn't courting her. When she opened the box, a second gasp escaped her, for inside were two mother-of-pearl hair combs. "How beautiful, but you shouldn't have. No doubt they were quite expensive." As if the gifts Weymouth had given her weren't ten times what the combs were worth.

"Perhaps." The major shrugged, as if it didn't matter. "I thought you might like to have something pretty for tonight but not garish, something that meant something instead of an empty offering from one of the men Johnathan wishes for you to meet." The intense look in his brown eyes made her shiver with anticipation and excitement. "However, these once belonged to my grandmother. I've kept them safe for years, never knowing what to do with them. Somehow, I knew they were destined for you, for no other woman in my life is worthy of them."

Oh, Cornelius, what am I to do with you?

With her heart squeezing and awareness of him dancing over her skin, she snapped the lid shut, but she didn't answer with words. Instead, she put a finger to her lips, took his free hand, and then led him out of the parlor and into the corridor beyond.

"Where are we going?" Confusion threaded through his inquiry.

Thank goodness for an empty hallway. "Upstairs to my rooms."

"But why?"

"You'll see." She hastened her pace and didn't slow until they were both safely behind her closed door. They'd not passed any of the servants during their passage.

"Penelope?"

A huff escaped to ruffle the curls on her forehead. She laid the box on her bureau then locked the door. "I intend to thank you in a way you'll understand." Then she crossed the bedroom floor to lock the adjoining door to the dressing room. "In the way that will make the greatest impression."

"Oh?" The major set the bouquet into an ornate vase that rested on a small table that sat near a window. "Why?"

"Because I have wasted far too much of my life doing things I had no interest in. Am I making up for lost time?" She continued to talk as she prowled over the floor toward him. "Perhaps, but I am also having the time of my life living out a fantasy I had as a young girl." When she reached his location, Penny shoved the greatcoat from his shoulders. It fell to the floor with a soft sigh. "And I want to see it through."

He peered down at her with amusement and desire warring for dominance in his eyes. Finally, Cornelius nodded. "I am yours to command, my lady, but be warned. If we are to couple this afternoon, it will prove frantic and chaotic, for I, too, am apparently living out... something borne from the shadows of my mind."

"Oh." Not knowing what that meant but battered from the waves of need crashing into her from his proximity, she manipulated the buttons of his jacket then shoved it off his shoulders and down his arms until it pooled on the floor. "Tell me you want me, Major. Tell me if things were different, you would have chosen me…" Then her voice broke and the bravado she had when trying to undress him faltered.

Dear heavens, Penny, you're far too bold for him, and you don't need a man besides.

That might be true, but she suspected she needed this one far more than was good for her.

"Damnation, woman, of course I would. Couldn't you guess from that afternoon in the hedge maze?" he asked as he tugged her into his arms.

"That was then. Years have passed, but if you weren't you and I wasn't me, would you still choose me above all others?" It was a convoluted question that danced around the truth, but she didn't care. She was a coward and didn't dare speak the words being etched onto her heart.

"God, yes." Then his lips were on hers, and the passion that provoked the kiss had the power to weaken her knees. When he wrenched away, he continued to remove clothing.

His waistcoat was the next article of clothing to land on the floor, quickly followed by his cuffs, collar, and cravat. When he stood in his lawn shirt, buff-colored breeches, and boots, another tremble tumbled down her spine.

There was something far too distracting about watching a handsome, somewhat broken man shed his clothing. Penny stared, for she suspected these little trysts couldn't last much longer. Her mouth went dry, which was odd, for that never happened to her. "Truly?"

"Yes." He shrugged. "Does the reason I wish to bed you, or rather let you seduce me, matter?"

"It does not." When she attempted to leave the bed in order to help him off with the remainder of this clothing, he had none of it.

The major caught her and tossed her back on that piece of furniture. His grin sent heat over her skin, and the wicked promise in his eyes had flutters sailing through her belly. "But know this, I *am* me and you *are* you, and *I* want *you* so damned much."

Oddly, that was the most romantic thing she'd ever heard. "Oh, goodness…"

"Indeed." His lips twitched but he didn't outright grin in amusement. Then he was on the bed with her, and she was in his arms; his kisses caught her by surprise. This time around, he was quite intense, and soon enough, she was lost on a sea of sensation that seemed far too large for her to try and contain.

So she didn't even try, for perhaps drowning would be good for her. Eventually, she wrenched away, merely to draw air into her lungs; he was much like a summer thunderstorm that came on suddenly. "Cornelius…"

"Hmm?" he asked against the skin at the crook of her shoulder.

"I need you." There was nothing else to say since the ability to think was rapidly leaving her.

"Good." As he spoke, he yanked down the bodice of her gown, bringing the underclothing with it with such strength she feared that he might tear the fabric. It was quite intoxicating.

Once her breasts were exposed, he wasted no time taking one mound in his hand to worry the nipple with a thumb and forefinger while latching onto her other hardened bud with his lips, teasing it with his tongue.

Wild sensation streaked through her body and pleasure circled through her lower belly. A soft moan escaped her. "Cornelius…" Why couldn't she give life to the words she truly wanted? She couldn't think, not when he was doing such wonderfully wicked things to her, but not content to just lie there, Penny plucked at the thin lawn of his shirt, tugging the tails from the waist of his breeches. "Let me touch you."

He grunted. "As I said, I'm yours to command." Then he continued his quest to separate her from reality.

Though it was all too much, Penny put her hands beneath his shirt and skimmed her palms up his chest. The mat of thick, coarse hair rasped against her skin and enhanced the need throbbing through her veins. When one of her fingertips glanced over a flat disc his nipple went immediately erect, and he hissed out a breath. Emboldened, she lifted her head to press her lips to the hollow of his throat.

Heavens, he smells so good!

"Temptress." The low rumble of his voice tickled through her chest. "I adore having your hands on me." Again, he turned his attention to her breasts, and she thought that stimulation would surely send her over that edge far too soon.

Her heartbeat raced. Heat flooded her body, but when he slipped a hand between her thighs, she was convinced she might expire from pleasure this time.

"You have no idea how many nights I dreamed of you while away in India, how many times I kept your face in my mind to help block out the unsavory things needed of me." When she relaxed, he put a knee between her legs and splayed her open while his brown gaze bored in hers. "At times, I was thoroughly convinced you were an angel."

"I'm sorry you had such a bad go of it while there." Yet it was lovely to hear those words. At least he hadn't forgotten her.

"It is what is expected of men in our world." His eyes were intense as he held her gaze with his fingers strumming over her sensitive folds. "I never thought I'd survive long enough to come home."

"Yet you did, and I'm glad." Before she could expand that thought or pluck words from the passionate haze in her brain, the major rubbed his fingertips over the swelling button at her center, and familiar sensations washed over her, around her, through her. "Oh goodness." She squirmed from his attentions, but he didn't let up. Trembles and tingles collected through her body; she clung to his shoulders, moved her hips in time to his ministrations and tried to press herself closer to him.

This is always my favorite part!

When a release caught her up in its vortex, she let out a half-stifled scream as her core quivered and pleasure raced through her. A certain shivering, enhanced need flowed through her, for she needed him in her body right this second. Now that he'd introduced her to this wonderful, carnal world that her husband had kept her from, she couldn't wait to linger there once more.

"Damn, but you look as if you've seen heaven," the major whispered as he removed himself from the bed.

"If I did, it wasn't complete, for you didn't join me." Was that revealing too much?

"Ah, Penny." He put down his frontfalls, and when his impressive, erect length tumbled out of his breeches, he took himself in hand, pumping his shaft as she watched, or perhaps *because* she watched. "You are far too good for me, I fear."

What did that mean?

The major grabbed her ankles, and when he tugged her to the edge of the bed, she squealed and was plunged into another sea of sensation. With a half grin, he balanced her hips there and shoved her legs into the air, spreading them wide as he did.

This was different, and before she could question him, he penetrated her body with a powerful thrust, and didn't stop until his hard, hot, thick length filled her passage. "Merciful heavens, that's wonderful."

"Different positions each come with their own advantages," he said around what sounded like a growl. Then he began to move within her, and Penny completely lost the ability to think, let alone remember her own name. Just like when he'd taken her from behind at the bookshop, she had no choice but to acclimate to this new way of intercourse.

And it was so very lovely.

Over and over he slammed into her, sinking his shaft deep, oh impossibly deep. His pushes were quick and hard, as if he had no intention of being gentle this time, and then his movements grew frantic, impulsive, yet that friction, that plunging sensation made her feel as if she were being hurtled into the great unknown.

"Cornelius... Oh, God..."

Another grunt and a tight grin. "Not a god, only just a mere major." He leaned over her while holding one of her legs, and with the other hand, he once more found that slippery button at her center and bedeviled it.

That was when she fractured, or more accurately, her body began to break a second time. It was almost as if she were coming apart at the seams as unbelievable pleasure shot through her body and burned through her blood. "Cornelius!" And she was lost on a sea of sensation, except she was thrust into a world that was absent of light and sound as her body shook, and her passage rocked with contractions.

With a muffled shout of his own, the major followed her into that sacred space on the heels of one last powerful stroke. He ground his pelvis into hers. Warmth filled her core. Seconds later, he pulled away, leaving her oddly bereft of his presence and with a lingering sense of disappointment.

"Oh." She couldn't help her frown. "I'd hoped it would have lasted longer."

"So did I, but I fear you make me far too randy to finesse such things." Yet his grin suggested he was as giddy as a schoolboy at Christmas. "Trust me, that *is* a good thing for a man my age." As he tucked his flaccid shaft back into his breeches and did up the buttons, Penny lay collapsed on the bed, her heartbeat and thoughts racing.

"You have completely changed how I've looked at bed sport," she finally managed to pant out. Residual tremors chased themselves up and down her spine. Would she ever have enough of him? Eventually, their trysts would need to end.

His grin stimulated her all over again. "I'll wager there are many things you don't know, least of all about me."

"Will you tell me? After all, haven't I earned the right to know?"

"Ha." Remarkably, his grin returned. "Perhaps you have, indeed. If we can ever be in each other's company without clothes coming off, then yes, I will tell you."

"Thank you." A grin of her own curved her lips. "However,

you need to go. I must ring for a bath then dress for dinner. Mama and Johnathan will be home soon from their errands." A sigh escaped, for this interlude had been lovely, and oddly, she felt closer to him than she ever had. "Will I see you at the rout tonight? After all, it *is* Valentine's Day?" The day set aside for lovers.

For us.

"Absolutely. I wouldn't miss it."

She nodded. "Try not to be seen as you leave, and thank you for the gifts."

"You are quite welcome." When he leaned down and kissed her forehead, her heart trembled.

Then he was gone, and she hugged a pillow to her chest. *Drat, drat, drat.* Perhaps Mrs. Potter was correct. Somehow, she'd fallen in love with her brother's best friend, and these feelings were no longer the infatuation from when she was a young woman. Surely, hoping for anything more than what they currently enjoyed together was folly, for he wasn't a forever sort of man, and she didn't want to marry again.

Did she?

CHAPTER FOURTEEN

Valentine's rout
Abbott House
Hanover Square, Mayfair
London

CORNELIUS MET BIRCHFIELD outside the drawing room. He nodded in greeting. "Where are the ladies tonight?" Not wishing to be too obvious in regard to Penny, he didn't mention her specifically by name.

"Mama saw a couple of friends, so she came up ahead of me. I assume Penny went with her." The earl shrugged. "Everywhere one turns tonight, there are reminders of love and romance in the décor. Makes a man wish to cast up his accounts."

"Indeed."

Though he snorted and agreed with his friend up to a point, he didn't mind the red-and-pink swags and bows made from tulle. As they moved into the crowded drawing room, hearts and Cupid silhouettes had been cut from foiled paper. Pink, red, and white roses decorated the room in vases set into floral groupings in each corner, along with potted ferns and other various plant life. Candles in silver holders as well as wall sconces added soft illumination to the space; spangles, beads, and jewels sparkled in that flickering light.

"Ah, there is Penny. She's speaking with the viscount I told you about yesterday."

With a frown, Cornelius sent his gaze about the room until he found the couple in question. His only interest was with Penny, who was even more stunning tonight than she'd been earlier in the afternoon when he'd called on her.

Her gown clearly had been chosen to ensure attention, whether his or someone else's Cornelius couldn't say, but the red silk with silver satin trim on the hem, waist, and bodice showed off her form to perfection. A silver necklace graced her slim neck, with a heart-shaped ruby dangling between her collarbones, but her blonde-brown hair, done in an elaborate undo with curls and braids caught his attention for no other reason than she'd placed the mother-of-pearl combs in those tresses.

It appeared the young viscount talked *at* her instead of *with* her, for the look of boredom on her face spoke volumes. When she glanced away, her gaze collided with Cornelius's, and her whole face illuminated with welcome. As it had the habit of doing these days, his world tilted. Sneaking around with Penny for no other reason than to play carnal games was by far the most fun he had in some time, yet there was more to their relationship than that. He looked forward to seeing her, talking with her, sharing little bits about his life with her, and hearing the same from her in return. When her eyes widened and she smiled in the special way she reserved only for him, he swore she might have fallen from heaven.

She gave him back a sense of calm and purpose that had been missing for more than a while in his life. It was pure insanity how well they interacted together, and if given the chance, he wanted to pursue more with her that had nothing to do with bed sport. The darling woman accepted him as he was, didn't demand anything of him, didn't want gifts, didn't wish to change him, and that meant… everything.

They were just who they were to each other. There was a certain amount of freedom there.

And as if he were a moth, he needed to bask in her light. "I'm going to say hello to your sister," he told Birchwood, not caring if he agreed or not. His feet carried him of their own accord, for he certainly didn't feel them on the floor. The moment he reached her side, he scooped up her hand and ferried it to his lips. "Lady Penelope, you are truly a vision tonight."

"And you, Major, are a charming rogue." A faint blush went through her cheeks as he held her hand a few seconds longer than politeness demanded. "However, you are quite handsome. I appreciate your pink waistcoat. It sets you apart from every other man tonight in the same dark evening clothes."

Before he could respond, Viscount Middleton cleared his throat. Then the bugger tried to move Penny away from him.

"If you don't mind, Major Montgomery, I was talking with the lady, so you'll need to wait your turn." An open challenge reflected in the younger man's hazel eyes, a sure sign that he had, indeed, asked Birchfield for permission to call on Penny as well as pay his addresses.

"Pish posh, Lord Middleton." She waved a hand in dismissal. Clearly, she wasn't impressed with the man. "There is plenty of time this evening to talk later. The major and I are old friends."

The viscount bristled. "That doesn't give him leave to interrupt—"

Penny frowned when a few people around them stared. "Lower your voice, Middleton. For shame." Bouncing her gaze between them, she said, "There are plenty of other ladies here tonight, and it's Valentine's Day. You needn't set the whole of your attention on me."

The expression on the viscount's face was like a thundercloud. "Will you promise me a dance later, then?"

"Of course, but for the time being, why don't you fetch me a glass of champagne?"

With a tight nod and a narrow-eyed gaze at Cornelius, the viscount left. Immediately, he was swallowed up the milling crowd filling the room.

Penny giggled, and the sound went straight to his stones. "He's rather a scare, isn't he?"

"Indeed." Suddenly nervous, knots pulled in his gut. Would he ultimately lose her to someone who held a decided place in the *beau monde*? Feeling quite daring, he came a bit closer and leaned his head down. With his lips to her ear, he said, "Meet me in our host's library if you wish for a bit of scandal tonight."

With a tiny gasp, she pulled away and peered up at him. "Truly?"

"Oh, yes." He nodded. In a barely audible whisper, he continued, "I'll leave first. Soon. You can follow in a quarter hour."

"Such lovely excitement and on Valentine's Day to boot!" Then she bit off a groan. "Lord Middleton has returned, but yes, I'll meet you."

"Until then." He slipped away before the viscount could navigate over to her.

When he reached the library on the lower level, shadows clung to the room. One candle burned on the mantle, for the expectation that guests would drift into this room was low. Just for his peace of mind, Cornelius padded about the room, his footsteps muffled by the thick Aubusson rugs covering the floor. It wouldn't do for someone else to be hiding, hoping for an assignation, who might inadvertently bear witness to what he wished to do with Penny.

Just as he finished his reconnaissance, the door opened, and the soft snick of the panel closing covered his footfalls as he returned across the room. Through the dim illumination, he discerned Penny's form while her eyes were still adjusting to the near darkness.

"I'm glad you decided to join me." Perhaps he was far too reckless, but when he was with her, his confidence soared, and he felt as if he could do anything if only she would smile at him. As soon as he was close, he took her into his arms.

"Why wouldn't I?" When she rested a hand on his chest, he swore that she might have scorched his skin through his clothing. "A handsome major, a dimly lit library filled with books, and scandal in the offing?"

"God, I love your penchant for plain speaking." Then he claimed her lips with his in a heated kiss that he hoped imprinted himself on her mind.

Don't forget me.

"You are always so potent," she whispered, then nipped a line of kisses beneath his jaw. "What am I going to do with you?"

Past this moment or twenty years in the future? He didn't have the courage to ask. "The possibilities are endless." Instead, he merely kissed her again, reveling in the softness of her skin and the faint floral scent of her. As he did so, he walked her backward until they were hidden in the shadows at the other end of the room away from the guttering candle.

She quickly divested herself of her gloves, abandoning them to the floor. "They are, but since I don't want to waste this moment, let's start." After wrenching his shirt tails from the waist of his evening breeches, she smoothed a hand over the expanse of his chest, and when she came to one of his nipples, she teased it into a hard bud by flicking it with a fingernail.

Immediate reaction streaked through his veins, for that exploration had caught him unawares. Tiny fires erupted in his blood. "Ah, Penelope, I fear you will kill me, for you have acclimated far too well to scandal."

"I hope not, for I want you around for a while yet." She tipped her chin upward until their gazes met. Mischief clouded her dark gray eyes. "Shall I continue?"

Interest shivered through his shaft as he remembered how her lush curves had felt nestled against his body. "God, yes."

"Good," she said in a barely there whisper, as she walked her fingers down his torso and then, after a slight pause, she brushed those fingers over his growing member that pressed urgently against the front of his breeches. "Hmm, how to begin…"

"Vixen." Damn but he was intrigued and aroused by her daring and initiative. After he removed his own gloves, he tossed them to the nearest chair.

"Ah, I know." With a wink, Penny dropped to her knees in

front of him. With fingers that trembled, she slowly worked each button from its hole at his frontfalls and then encouraged the placket down. When his rapidly engorging shaft sprang out, she gasped then grinned up at him.

"You are going to devour me, aren't you?"

"Oh, yes. I'm so excited that I finally have the opportunity to familiarize myself with your equipage." Tentatively, she traced a fingertip along the side of his member.

Fuck!

The light touch paired with her tart mouth and curious nature made her irresistible. "I think I've corrupted you." For a few seconds, he watched her in the shadows. The guttering candle flame across the room sent eerie shadows over the walls.

"Or you've opened a new world for me, one which was stolen from me by my husband's negligence." She wrapped her hand about his stiffening length, but it was her words that made him so randy. "For that, I can never repay you."

"There is no need, of course. I'm merely happy that you are." The realization struck him like a blow. At the core of what was between them, he just wanted to see her happy.

"Yes, well, let's hope I can do this with some confidence. Performing fellatio is quite new for me." On a first, unsure stroke, she frowned. "I adore how hard you are, how large you grow." Then she held him more firmly and drew her curled fingers up and down his shaft.

Bloody hell. He sucked in a sharp breath, for her fumbling strokes and caresses had awareness and need shivering along his spine faster than the touch of an experienced courtesan. "Let me help you start." Gently, so she wouldn't think he tried to take control, he settled his hand over hers, showed her how to hold his length to maximum advantage. "Go slowly at first, else everything will end in a mess and embarrassment."

After a few minutes of experimentation, a faint smile curved her lips. "So fascinating. I can't wait to taste you." Soon she was stroking his flesh as if she'd been doing it all her life. Up and down her fingers went. Combined with a few gentle squeezes and the sensation of her nails against that sensitive flesh, strong reaction careened through his member.

And with every pass, he hardened further. Need tingled in his stones, but just when he suggested she stop, the cheeky woman cupped his testicles in her other hand, squeezed them with a firm insistence that had his eyes ready to cross.

"Enjoying yourself?" she asked as she glanced up at him with shining eyes in the shadows.

"Yes, but perhaps we should stop here."

"Mmm, where is the scandal in that?" One of her light-brown eyebrows rose in challenge, then with a husky chuckle, she leaned forward and closed her rosy lips around the head of his shaft.

Shit, shit, shit!

Cornelius's whole body jerked as if it had come awake with a shock. She giggled, and the vibrations buzzed around his length, enhancing the exquisite torture she'd already given him. While holding his stones in her hand, Penny moved closer to him and slowly she took his member into her mouth as far as he could go until his tip hit the back of her throat.

Then, she swallowed, and the contracting muscles gently squeezed his prick. He nearly shot his wad right there, but he bore down on the urge and gritted his teeth.

"Penny…"

She drew off his shaft with a slight pop. "I could rather grow to adore pleasuring you like this." At least she released his stones, and he knew a moment's relief, but it was short-lived, for she slipped that hand around the back of his thigh and took him once more into the warm cavern of her mouth.

Perhaps he'd already died and gone to heaven, for there were no words he could summon. In seconds, he was lost in the wonder that was his not-so-innocent but far-too-wicked lover as she proceeded to suck him off.

It took her a few seconds to find a rhythm, but once she did, he was surely consigned to death. As he remained helpless in her hold, she worked him over with both her hand and her mouth. When she swirled her tongue beneath the head of his shaft, how she added shivering sensation by scraping her nails along the side of his shaft, the strength nearly left his legs.

How damned fortunate am I to have found her in the bookshop?

Then his mind began to shatter. With a groan, he buried his hands in her soft hair, tangled his fingers in those tresses and because he needed to, Cornelius thrust gently into her mouth.

For one fleeting moment, she paused. Confusion flashed in her eyes, but then she accepted the new addition, and her fingers delved tighter into the flesh of his thigh. The faster and deeper he thrust, the more frantic and harder she worked him over, and the sight of her blonde head with his grandmother's combs bobbing on his shaft was enough to hurtle him over the point of no return.

Warning tingled through his stones. His muscles bunched and stiffened. At the last second, just before his release jetted out of him, he pulled out of Penny's mouth. The stream of come splattered against the back of a leather sofa. While she watched with rounded eyes, he took himself in hand to finish the job, and with a groan, he sagged and rested a shoulder to the nearest bookshelf.

"Damn, that was good."

She frowned. "Why did you not let me swallow?"

"You are not my whore, Penelope, and neither is this the time or place for such things." When she would have protested, he shook his head and stuffed his flagging shaft back into this evening breeches. "If that is something you'd like to experience, we'll do it again in private." Quickly, he did up the buttons of his frontfalls. "It's no one else's business but our own." And he wanted such a thing to be special, sacred, if it could even be called that. "I'm afraid I didn't explain myself well." Seconds later, he took his handkerchief out and gave the back of the sofa a bit of a wipe down, so it wasn't so obvious what had occurred.

Standing, she brushed a piece of lint from her skirts. "You are a dear, dear man," she said in a whisper, closed the distance between them, and then drew his head down for a gentle, lingering kiss. "No wonder the female population of London vies for your favor."

"I am not spending Valentine's night with them, am I?" Though he kissed her, what he truly wanted was to spirit her away from this house, take her home, and spend the rest of the night showing her what he was too cowardly to say. Then he maneuvered her over the floor until her back hit the bookshelf behind her. "Let me return the favor for you."

A gasp escaped her. "Do you mean to put your mouth on me?"

"Yes."

"But you already did that in the bookshop a few days ago. Wasn't that enough for you?"

How adorable was she? A queer little flutter moved through his mouth. "It is never enough when a banquet is presented to a starving man, and you are the sweetest delicacy I have tasted." So saying, he dropped to his knees in front of her. "Gather your skirts and hook one of your knees over my shoulder."

The look she bestowed upon him as she followed instructions had the power to turn his blood molten. "I always thought you represented adventure whenever I thought of you so far away from England, and I was right. I can barely catch my breath around you."

"Good." He rather liked that metaphor. When she was completely open for him, he spent the next several moments strumming his fingers along her folds slick with arousal, and when he brought that all-important bundle of nerves out of hiding at her center, she gasped again. Trembles went through her thighs and transferred to him, prompting a grin. "It's flattering to know you want me so much."

"Do shut up, Major, and make me fly." The waspish tone betrayed just how frustrated she was from the delay.

"As my lady wishes." Then he set to work suckling that slippery bud while caressing his fingers along her flesh, using a finger to flirt in and out of her passage.

The sounds of pleasure and encouragement she made spurred him onward. One of her hands went into his hair, urging him closer to her body. When he found a rhythm and used some creativity in his pleasuring, she moved her hips to better receive the thrusts from his tongue and fingers.

"Oh…" Her breathing came in fast pants each time he rubbed his tongue frantically and insistently over her nubbin; her head lolled onto her shoulder as one of her hands wandered beneath her bodice to fondle a nipple.

Damn, but that was one of the most erotic things he'd ever seen. His shaft stirred with interest again, and he worked all the faster to send her over the edge.

"Cornelius, dear heavens, almost…. Almost!" A shiver racked her body, and just when he anticipated watching her go over the edge, the door to the library slammed open hard enough that it bounced off the wall.

"Penelope Anne, for shame!" The utterance came from Birchfield, and when the earl came further into the room, she gasped and immediately removed herself from Cornelius's person. "Major Montgomery, what the hell are you doing to my sister?" The thunderous inquiry echoed off the walls and bookshelves.

"Well, fuck," he murmured and then slowly climbed to his feet. Before he turned around, Cornelius retrieved his handkerchief from his waistcoat pocket and then wiped his face. As he faced the earl, his confidence wavered, for he was also presented with the dowager countess as well as Viscount Middleton, each wearing various degrees of shock in their expressions. With a quick glance at Penny, who had tears in her eyes, knots pulled in his belly for putting her into this position. Deliberately, he moved in front of her, blocking her from their judgment. Tucking his hands behind his back, he waved the handkerchief, and nodded when she took it from him. "Damn, Birchfield, you could have at least waited thirty seconds for the lady to finish."

"I came to retrieve my sister," the earl explained with a reddened face. "When she left the drawing room, I suspected she'd retreat to the library since she has an affinity for books. I had no idea you'd be here defiling her."

The dowager spoke next. She clutched a hand to her chest. "That I would live long enough to see my daughter behaving like a common trollop," she managed in a choked whisper.

From behind him, Penny snorted. "That assumes there is an uncommon variety of trollops out there. Perhaps I'm one of them."

"Terrible girl." Then the older woman's eyes rolled back in her head, and she slumped to the library floor.

"Shit." Birchfield glared at him. "Help me move my mother to one of the sofas."

"Of course." Cornelius sprang into action. He scooped up the dowager's feet while Johnathan lifted her beneath the arms. Between the two of them, they moved her dead weight to the closest leather sofa and made her as comfortable as they could. "If you want me to apologize for what you just saw, I won't. We are both consenting adults, and she is a widow."

Viscount Middleton cleared his throat. In the illumination coming into the room from a sconce in the corridor, his face was red with either anger or embarrassment. "What sort of betrayal is this, Birchfield?" He shoved a hand through his hair. "I refuse to marry your sister if she is this fast, and I don't want used goods besides."

"Good heavens, what a nodcock." Penny peered around Cornelius's shoulder. "If you thought I was an innocent, you're an arse. I'm a widow. What do you think that has entailed?"

Middleton frowned. "Be that as it may, I don't want his cast offs."

"Well, good luck with that, then," she shot off, because she could never curb that tart mouth he adored. "From the gossip, the major has been with a good percentage of the female members of the *beau monde*."

The viscount glared at Birchfield. "I'll have the dowry couriered to you tomorrow. Good night."

Throughout the odd exchange, Cornelius bit the inside of his cheek to prevent laughing at the Drury Lane affair.

"Middleton, wait!" As Birchfield strode to the door, the viscount never broke stride. Then the earl turned on Cornelius. "How dare you destroy her chances of making a decent match. I told you to stay away from her!"

Before he could defend himself, another couple drifted into the room. Unfortunately, it was their host and hostess of the evening, both looking concerned and confused.

Birchfield ignored them. "I ought to call you out for what you've done."

"Oh, do stop, Johnathan." Penny stepped around Cornelius. "I'm a widow, so therefore I can't be ruined. Beyond that, I know my own mind, and now that I have the freedom to do so, I'm doing things that benefit me."

"Like whore yourself out to a man who has made it a priority to fuck half the women in London, eligible or not?"

"Language, Birchfield," she said, with eyes flashing blue-gray fire as she propped her hands on her hips.

"Not well done of you, Birchfield." A wave of heated anger welled in Cornelius's chest. "What is between the lady and me is none of your business."

The earl rounded on him with his hands curled into fists. "I told you my sister was not for you!"

This was ridiculous. "That's too bad, because I'm quite a decent fellow, and I thought that, as your best friend, you could see that."

"Penny is too good for you!" Then Birchfield sprang at him with such force that they both crashed to the floor while Penny moved over to the sofa where the dowager had just come 'round from her faint.

For the next few minutes, blows and punches were exchanged between him and Birchfield. His fists found purchase more than a few times, and the earl returned the volleys until they'd both have bruises on the morrow. When his bottom lip became busted and the metallic taste of blood flooded his mouth, it only enraged him more, so he retaliated by landing a facer to his best friend. The familiar crunch of cartilage followed, for Birchfield's nose was broken.

"Stop this at once, both of you!" Penny attempted to separate them, but they paid her no mind. She stamped a foot. "This is juvenile."

"Enough!" Birchfield landed Cornelius a punch that knocked him onto his back. He staggered to his feet and peered down at him with blood dripping down his face. "Keep your damned hands off my sister," he demanded, in a winded voice.

Pain moved through his head and body as he sat up. "I can't do that."

"Why the hell not?" Birchfield held his folded handkerchief to his streaming nose.

Cornelius didn't know if it was the fight, what he'd shared with Penny, the drama of the evening, or the fact it was Valentine's Day, but it was time for a few truths to come out. "Because I'm almost certain I'm in love with her. What's more, I believe I have been in fits and starts since I left to serve out my commission."

"What?" Birchfield stared.

"What?" The dowager collapsed against the decorative pillows as she watched the proceedings.

"What?" Shock threaded through Penny's utterance as she fell to her knees at his side. With a hand to his forehead and concern in her eyes, she asked, "Are you quite well? Did he scramble your brains just now?"

"No." A chuckle left his throat, but pain went through Cornelius's head. "Truth to tell, this is the sanest I've been in many years."

Would that be enough to usher in the next phase of his life? With her? Only time would tell.

CHAPTER FIFTEEN

WHAT IS HAPPENING?

Penny stared at the major and the wreck of his face from fighting with her brother. "You are in love with me?" How often had she dreamed about this exact moment over the years? Now that it was finally here, it seemed far too surreal, especially following the events of the past twenty minutes.

Mr. Abbott cleared his throat. With a frown, Penny glanced across the room at the gray-haired man who stood beside his elegant wife, whose snow-white hair was simply gorgeous and set off the delicate silver and sapphire tiara sitting atop those tresses. "Perhaps you should explain, Major. After that spectacular fight, it isn't good form for a man to say something as shocking as you did without further preamble."

"Perhaps you are correct, and we *did* interrupt your rout."

"Pish posh." Mrs. Abbott waved a gloved hand. Sapphires from her necklace glimmered in the low light. "This is much more entertaining, and I have always maintained that if there wasn't some sort of scandal on Valentine's Day, then something is amiss." She grinned at her husband. "After all, we were matched on this day years ago, so it holds a special spot in our lives."

"That is quite true." Mr. Abbott touched her hand. "Allow me to light more candles. I have a feeling the story we're in for will prove quite juicy."

Penny bounced her gaze from her brother as he glared while attempting to stem his bloody nose, to her mother, who looked at the proceedings with interest due to her penchant for theatrics, then back to Cornelius who watched her with an odd expression on his face. "I, uh, think we should get off the floor."

"Perhaps." But Cornelius chuckled as he tucked his shirttails back into his breeches. "Though this is the least scandalous thing we've done tonight."

"Do stop," she whispered with heat in her cheeks. After she scrambled to her feet, she assisted him into a standing position, which he accomplished with a groan. "Where is your cane?"

"Oh." He frowned. "I believe I inadvertently left it in the drawing room, but it matters not. I don't plan to do much walking just now. At least not until after I tell you what's been on my mind for a couple of days."

"This is ridiculous," Johnathan said as he tucked his bloodied handkerchief into an interior pocket of his tailcoat. Drops of blood speckled his cravat and collar. "It doesn't matter what the major has to say. This evening is concluded for us. Come, Penny. I'm taking you and Mama home. We've all been overstimulated."

For one horrible moment, she was tempted to follow his dictates, for she feared what Cornelius would say, and perhaps he'd planned to do so for all the wrong reasons, but the other part of her brain was curious, for she'd secretly hoped for just this since she'd been a young woman of fifteen. Then she shook her head.

"No."

"I beg your pardon?"

As Mr. Abbott lit candles about the room and the shadows retreated, her confidence grew. "All my life I've followed the rules, or did what some man told me to do. First it was Papa, then my husband, and now you. And while the three of you thought you had my best interests at heart, you really meant you didn't know what to do with me. You took the easy way out, swept me beneath the proverbial rug, so I was out of sight and out of mind."

"That's not—"

She held up a hand. "It is, and you know it. Since becoming a widow, I decided to make my own decisions. Working at the bookshop was merely one of them." With a shrug, she continued. "Weymouth left me well off, and I mean to keep exploring the things that interest me. When Major Montgomery randomly came into the bookshop a handful of days ago, he was something I wished to pursue."

"Despite my opposition." It wasn't a question as her brother crossed his arms at his chest.

"Yes." Penny nodded. "I truly believe there is something between us."

"It's called scandal, and I won't allow it to continue." Johnathan was nothing if not consistent. "Even Mama is opposed to you having anything to do with the major."

When she glanced over, her mother was busy rubbing at a spot on her skirts. "Oh, Johnathan. Can you not see that I'm a woman grown and capable of living my life as I wish? I'm no longer your little sister who needs protection. Whether my life is fully emersed in scandal or not isn't your concern. I know my own mind, and I will weather the consequences of my actions as they occur."

Though I rather hope I don't need to.

"I… I suppose I *do* have a tendency to think of you still as a young woman," Johnathan said with a frown. "I apologize."

Finally, Cornelius cleared his throat. "If I may speak now?" When everyone in the room stared at him, a bit of ruddy color sneaked up his neck over his cravat. "After all, I believe we might be able to move forward from this night afterward."

"Fine." Her brother gave a curt nod. "Say what you will, then get the hell out of our lives."

The knots of worry in Penny's belly pulled. "You don't mean that, Johnathan. He is your best friend and has been since before I was even born."

"That was before he decided to compromise you," he said from what sounded like around gritted teeth.

She ignored him to focus on the major. "You'd best speak while you can. Johnathan's mercurial mood might change in the next minute." Additionally, her curiosity might get the better of her if she didn't hear what he wished to say.

"This is true." As he held her gaze with his, he took a deep breath then let it ease out. "What I said to your brother after the fight was also true. I'm in love with you."

Again, she stared at him just as she had during that first moment. "Why would you think that? I thought what you and I were sharing was merely a winter's tryst."

"It was. Or at least it began as such."

"What the devil?" Her brother collapsed onto the arm of a leather, wingback chair as shock came over his face. "The two of you have been trysting? Right under my nose?"

Cornelius snorted. "Well, I rather doubt you wanted to watch."

Though Penny giggled, and even Mr. Abbott's lips twitched in amusement, Johnathan's glare strengthened. "Hush, Birchfield. It is not your turn to talk." Then she laid a hand on the major's arm. "Please continue."

"Right." He nodded, and even with the purpling bruises on his face and the blood dried on his chin from his broken bottom lip, he was still the most handsome man at the rout. "When I peeked through that bookshop window and saw you, I was immediately beset with memories from the past. That last night we were together before I left to serve in the military was the last perfect moment I had… until I stood at the bookshop window."

More sputtering came from her brother. "What the hell did the two of you get up to before he left for the military?"

Everyone in the room ignored him this time.

"I rather doubt either of those nights were perfect." But her heart was already fluttering like mad from his words.

"They were because you featured heavily in both." When Cornelius took one of her hands, she trembled. "Before we go further, I'm compelled to make certain you know that I'm not the man I was years ago. Hell, I'm not the man I was just two weeks ago."

"That doesn't matter; I was tip over tail for you all those years ago. In fact, I thought you hung the moon, but I didn't think you would ever notice me since I was eight years your junior, and Johnathan always had some issue or another with you being in my company."

"Because he always had his wick dipped into a different woman each month," her brother inserted, with heavy sarcasm in his voice.

They both frowned at him.

Cornelius squeezed her fingers. "While that was true, I'm not that man any longer. In fact, the only woman I want in my life from this moment forward is you." Before she could respond, he quickly continued. "After the military, I was adrift and lost. There were many reasons for that, and I'm trying to work through my mental failings, but it's slow going." He paused to perhaps think over his next words. "I need the support of a strong woman to help me through."

"Oh." She swallowed heavily to force moisture into her suddenly tight throat. "You believe I am that woman?"

"I do." With earnestness in his expression, he nodded. "Since you came back into my life, I have been enormously impressed with your gentleness, but also your determination to carve an existence for yourself that you're proud and content with. The more we've been together, the more I'm utterly captivated by you."

"That's so romantic," she breathed, as a tremble went down her spine.

"Somehow, I rather doubt you are even capable of developing feelings for any woman, let alone my sister," Birchfield said, with skepticism in his voice.

"Do hush, Birchfield," Mrs. Abbott said with a slight frown. "Love has the power to change everyone. Let him continue, at least."

"Thank you, Mrs. Abbott." The major nodded. When he put his gaze back on Penny, he dropped to one knee before her. "Do you remember this?" He withdrew something from his waistcoat pocket, and when he held it up, she gasped again, for it was the ring she'd fashioned for him all those years ago from a braided lock of her hair.

"You kept it after all this time?"

"Of course I did."

"I had such a crush on you back then," she admitted in a whispered voice. "I didn't expect you to take it seriously or even keep the trinket, but I wanted to give you something in remembrance of me before you went away."

"As if I could ever forget you." While still holding her gaze, he put the ring of her hair on the fourth finger of his right hand. "At that time, you were quite young; there was nothing I could do about it then, and I didn't want to extract a promise from you that you couldn't keep, especially since your brother had said your father wanted Weymouth for you."

"But that wasn't what I wanted for my life," she said, as tears welled in her eyes.

"And I didn't want you to wait for me in the event I didn't survive my time in India." He caught her hand in his again. "The final rebellion I was sent into to quell was the last time I remained in India, for I received a slice of a cutlass to my back—"

"The scar you wouldn't let me explore…"

"Yes." He nodded. "The blow knocked me from my horse, which is how I broke my ankle. I was bandaged and set as best they could do, but ultimately, they put me on a ship bound for home, and it was a long journey indeed, for I contracted a fever, was told I was in a bad state for weeks. Being on a ship for so long didn't help."

Shock roiled through her body. "I didn't know that."

"In those feverish imaginings, I dreamed of you. Honestly, I truly believe seeing you in those horrid times is what kept me grounded to this world, for I continued to hope I might have a chance, even if you were still married, so I continued to dream, spoke to you in those imaginings…"

"Oh, Cornelius." Her hand trembled in his, but she clung to his fingers. "I'm so grateful you didn't succumb to your injuries." And she was. That wasn't a lie. Then she removed one of the silver rings on her right hand. "You gave me this ring after I gave you mine. Do you remember?"

"Yes." He nodded and took it from her. "My father gifted me this when I went to university." The scrollwork had become a bit worn from age, but the metal shone bright, for she was careful to polish it every week. "I was so moved when you offered me your gift, so after we met in the hedge maze that night, I wanted— needed—you to remember me, had the silly hope that there might be a future for us if fate was kind."

"I wanted that too."

Her brother bristled. "You defiled my sister before she married the marquess?"

"Not quite." Cornelius snorted. "But there was scandal."

A grin tugged at the corners of Penny's lips. "And not in the way you think."

The major once more caught her hand. "Penelope, my sweetest dream, I believe that fate has put us both here now for a reason. Will you make me the happiest of men and promise to be my wife?"

"Oh, heavens." Despite the race of her heartbeat, despite the fact she had yearned quite hard for this exact moment, tears filled her eyes and spilled to her cheeks. "I hadn't planned to marry again, at least not right now, for I wanted to explore that freedom."

He gasped and stared at her with shock in his eyes. "You are rejecting me, then, after everything we've shared this week?"

"I…" Was she? This was the pinnacle of everything she'd ever wanted. And he was certainly quite delicious when it came to carnal pursuits, but was that enough? Did they share anything else between them? And would she only be in his life to calm his demons? "I..."

Mrs. Abbott came forward a few steps. "Lady Penelope, the poor man deserves an answer."

"Of course he does." She flicked her gaze to his dear face, upturned and waiting for her response. Clearly, he had honor since he'd served England in the war, and he was brave and strong for the same reasons. But her brother was right. He'd warmed beds all over England for many years. Would he prove faithful to just one or would he grow bored? Yet he'd remembered all the little things she'd told him thus far and even from the past, and she wore his grandmother's hair combs, which had stolen her heart when he'd offered them. "Oh, Cornelius, I've waited so long for you to say those words to me..."

"And?"

"I don't know that I want to be under another man's control or treated as if I'm his property." Her voice faltered. "I have dreams—"

"I know, and I want to help you fulfil them."

She frowned. "I don't want to become some man's arm or- nament to further his intentions or help him climb in society."

"Sweeting, have you ever known me to be that?"

"I don't know you all that well, but no." Slowly, she shook her head, for her heart was fairly seething at her brain. "You've been so sweet and romantic to me this week, but I don't want you to offer for me based on obligation from what happened between us. I..." She wiped away a tear. "I want you to want me *for* me, not because of something else."

"What the hell happened between the two of you this week?" her brother wanted to know, but everyone ignored him.

Again.

"Well, I'm not down on one knee on Valentine's night out of obligation." A trace of annoyance went through his expression.

"That's probably true." Was she being a fool?

"Penelope, I'm falling tip over tail into love with you. You've managed to capture my heart when I wasn't expecting it." His Adam's apple bobbed with a hard swallow. Moisture welled in his eyes, making the brandy hue more pronounced. "No one else has ever managed to get past my walls and find out the real man I hide… and no other woman has had the courage to love me for me despite all of that… until you."

Her chest tightened even as her heart squeezed. If she ever wanted the life she'd always dreamed of, she needed to be honest with herself. "This ring?" Gently, she removed her hand from his and tapped a fingertip to the remaining silver band on her right index finger. A plain silver band with a flat, square shape where there used to be a silver lion, but it had long since fallen off, and she'd lost it. "This came from Weymouth, one of his signet rings he gave me midway through our marriage when it was obvious we were merely existing with each other."

"What has that to do with me?"

"I keep wearing this to remind me that surface looks are deceptive."

He frowned. "Yet you kept my ring as well."

"Yes. I did, because to me it represents hope and a future unfulfilled."

"Meaning?" Expectation reflected in his eyes.

Flutters moved through her lower belly. "Meaning I have worn this ring every day since you gave it to me because…" She pressed her lips together; it was hopeless to deny what she felt for this man. "Because I am in love with you too. I worried and wondered what became of you after our letters stopped." She glanced over at her mother, whose cheeks reddened. "I never stopped hoping that eventually our paths would cross again."

"While those words are romantic, I need you to answer my question."

"I know." She nodded as she slowly sank to her knees in front of him. "I told you that I liked books because they never disappoint me, and I have never had that same feeling from any other person in my life."

"I remember."

"I adore books more than anything, so when I tell you that I also love you, please don't take that for granted. However, I also wish to move forward in opening my own bookshop once Mr. Chandler closes his. It's important to me that books are available to the public, because reading is rebellion and words are power."

"Sweeting, are you not listening? I have no intention of stopping you from doing anything. Loving someone means loving every part of them and what they stand for." He chuckled then winced. No doubt his injuries were paining him. "I don't want to tame you or quell your spirit. I refuse to demand that you suddenly become a proper member of society, for I adore you just as you are, but please, for the love of God, will you marry me?"

"Have we already wasted too much time?"

"As we're doing now?" He huffed. "Penny!" The word came out on a strangled sort of sound.

"I apologize." But she nodded as tears spilled onto her cheeks. "Yes, I will marry you." Then she tumbled into his arms and surrendered with a tiny sigh when he sought her lips with his. As she slipped her arms about his shoulders and pressed herself further into his embrace, her brother sputtered.

"Damn it, Penny, he's not good enough for you!"

"Oh, I know," she said, against the major's mouth. "That's one of the reasons he's perfect."

"He won't be able to take care of you in the style to which you've been accustomed over the years."

"He doesn't need to. Weymouth left me well off. We shall be fine, and besides," she turned her head and looked at her brother, "I'm hoping he can give me what the marquess never could."

"What is that?" he asked, as he crossed his arms at his chest while their mother pretended to faint again on the sofa.

"Children."

Mrs. Abbott sighed. She stepped close to her husband, who

slipped an arm around her waist. "Do shut up, Birchfield. This is turning into quite the romantic night."

"I fear I don't know what to do with myself," Cornelius whispered, as he slipped the silver band he'd given her years ago onto the fourth finger of her left hand. "I'll give you a proper ring later."

"That isn't necessary; I only want you." She'd crawl into his lap if there weren't so many people about. "I've only ever wanted you."

His eyes lit as he held her head between his hands. "My sentiment, exactly."

She smiled, and for the first time in many years, she was light, happy… free. Perhaps she did need to marry again after all. But there was one more thing she needed to do. Standing, Penny crossed the floor and stood in front of her brother. "Please don't be cross. Cornelius is your best friend; the two of you need each other, and I need you too. Don't shut us out just because we fell in love despite the odds and your opposition." Laying a hand on his arm, she added, "At least this time, I'm marrying for love."

A series of emotions went over her brother's face, but finally, he nodded as Cornelius joined her. "I only ever wanted what was best for you, Little Sister."

"And the best is Cornelius. You know it deep down."

His gaze flicked to her fiancé. "Perhaps I do, but—"

"No." Penny shook her head. "He is, and he'll take care of me, protect me… love me. Please celebrate with us."

"Damn, sometimes I think you are wiser than all of us." Then her brother tugged her into his arms and hugged her. "Congratulations. To you both."

Breathing deeply, she nodded against his shoulder. Finally, she was where she belonged, and perhaps this time, she wouldn't feel so alone.

CHAPTER SIXTEEN

May 1, 1817
Wilmington House
No. 23 Hanover Place
Mayfair, London

"DEAR GOD, I can hardly stand the wait," Cornelius whispered to Johnathan, as he paced the length of his soon-to-be in-laws' drawing room despite the twenty or so guests that assembled to bear witness to this special event.

Finally, it was his wedding day, the day he'd marry the love of his life, Lady Penelope, and yet he couldn't shake the crawling nerves or the twin tremors of excitement and worry that twisted up his spine. He touched the knot of his cravat to make certain it was straight. Then he tugged at the bottom of his waistcoat, done in a cheerful ice blue embroidered with vines and tulips. It *was* spring, after all. Then he moved a hand to the pocket of his waistcoat, checking to make sure he'd remembered to bring the ring with him. Was his hair correctly styled? He'd recently had it trimmed at the barber. Did the expertly tailored tailcoat fit him as it should?

Birchfield snickered. "You've waited all of two and a half months for this day. A handful of minutes isn't going to kill you."

"I rather think I've waited over thirteen years for this day, and the past two and a half months have been nigh unbearable." He glanced at the people laughing and chatting in rows of rented, delicate gilt chairs brought in for the occasion. Though his best friend had slowly come 'round to the prospect of him marrying Penny, Birchfield hadn't spoken to him for a few weeks after the scandal on Valentine's night.

Beyond that, Penny's family had kept her under constant vigilance and company, so he hadn't been allowed time alone with her over and above what they found at the bookshop, and even then, they'd only come together physically once, for the Chandlers were putting things to right ahead of the sale of the shop.

Now he desperately wanted a return of that intimacy with his soon-to-be wife.

"You've truly tossed your hat over the windmill for her, haven't you?" Birchfield asked in a whisper, as he regarded Cornelius with interest in his eyes.

"I am." And he didn't care who knew it. His chest tightened with happiness. "Which is why I'm tired of waiting," he replied and resumed his pacing. "I am more than ready to bring my bride home."

My bride. My heart.

The drawing room windows had been thrown open, and a sweet breeze redolent with the scents of flowers moved through the space where an abundance of fresh flower arrangements graced tables, the mantel, and the windowsills. The floral displays gave the room a cheerful air, and with the May Day sun shining in through the windows, the effect was rather magical.

A fresh start with new beginnings.

"I understand that, but it's not as if you've been completely cut off from her." Amusement hung in his voice and sparkled in Birchfield's eyes. "You've merely been made to act with decorum instead of scandal."

"Right, but do you know what it's been like to not touch her, kiss her, show her how much I adore her the past two and a half months?" he asked in a whisper, while struggling to contain his excitement and anxiety. His palms began to sweat, but he resisted the urge to wipe them on his evening breeches.

"You have become quite a romantic, Cornelius." Birchfield clapped a hand to his shoulder. "I'm sorry I resisted for so long, for I believe you are the perfect husband for my sister. You complement each other. It's my fondest hope she will help you sort out the mire of your mind."

"As do I." He peered out of the window while rustling fabric behind him betrayed that even more guests had arrived. "And Birchfield?"

"Hmm?"

"Please consider finding your own romance. I couldn't bear it if this world was deprived of your presence." The one thing marring the engagement period had been the fact that his best friend struggled with the demons terrorizing his own mind. He met the earl's gaze. "Promise me you will continue the fight."

The other man swallowed hard. "I promise I will do what I can."

"Good." Cornelius nodded. "I know it's difficult, but we all need to look after each other, and I refuse to go through the next portion of my life without you." Damn the war who stole the friend that he used to know. Along with the earl's responsibilities, the last two years had taken a toll on him.

Instead of answering in the same vein, Birchfield said, "It's time."

"Shit." He tightened his hand on the ivory head of his cane. "Do you think I'm good enough?"

The earl grinned, but the gesture didn't reach his eyes. "Quite."

"Thank you." Cornelius came to rest beside his best friend and glanced eagerly over the assembled guests. Many of his friends were there, as well as members of the *ton*. Plenty of Penny's friends came as well. When his gaze landed on Penny's mother, he gave her a nod and a small smile. She'd eventually come around to the fact that her daughter wouldn't be marrying a titled man this second time around, for planning the wedding had kept her quite busy.

But the only person he wished to see this morning was Penny.

Then the double doors to the drawing room opened. A clergyman of perhaps fifty or some odd years entered and strode up the aisle between the rows of guests. He nodded and smiled at various people, and when he reached the spot where Cornelius and Birchfield stood, he halted.

"Which one of you is the fortunate man about to marry one of the most beautiful women I've just seen in the corridor?"

"I am." His voice sounded weak and rusty, so Cornelius cleared his throat. "That would be me. I'm Major Montgomery." With nerves tying knots in his gut, he leaned his cane against the fireplace.

"Pleased to meet you." The clergyman nodded. He transferred a much-used copy of the *Book of Common Prayer* to his left hand and stuck out his right. "I'm Mr. Anders. Lady Penelope asked that I perform the ceremony. We've met a few times through various charities and causes." He gestured with his chin to a youngish man standing at the back of the room near the doors. "Mr. Podge is the parish clerk who'll make certain the register is signed, and I see you have more than enough witnesses."

"Yes." Cornelius nodded. He looked at the earl, who winked and then went to sit on the chair next to his mother. "You said she's in the corridor?" he asked the clergyman, when she still didn't appear.

"Oh, yes. We chatted a bit, and she's quite excited for today." The older man smiled. Genuine pleasure lit his hazel eyes. "She'll be along soon, I'd imagine."

"I'm living for that moment." He clasped his hands behind his back and trained his gaze on the drawing room doors. Then she was there, pausing long enough for him to feast his eyes on her form, and damn if he forgot how to breathe. "She's a vision and well worth the wait," he whispered and pressed a hand to his wildly beating heart.

Beside him, the clergyman chuckled.

Penny met his gaze with sparkling eyes. The smile she bestowed upon him nearly knocked him off his feet. Clad in a gown of bright raspberry-pink silk, she moved with grace and elegance as she came into the room. The frock's scalloped neckline drew his attention to the tops of her breasts while silver scrolling stitchwork lined the bodice, the flounced hem, as well as the short, puffed sleeves. A flush of excitement stained her pale cheeks, and her blonde-brown hair, dressed in a low chignon at the nape of her neck, gleamed. A posey of sweet Williams in a yellow hue and pink rose buds was tucked among the tresses over the loose knot, and he breathed a sigh of relief, for she'd chosen to wear the posey he'd sent over the night before.

"You're right, Mr. Anders. I'm extremely fortunate, and I hope I always remain deserving of her," he whispered when he found his voice again. Then she joined him, and the ability to concentrate flew right out of his head. "Hullo, sweeting."

"Good morning, Major." Amusement and excitement glimmered in the blue-gray depths of her eyes. She waved to Mr. and Mrs. Chandler, who, of course, had come to see her wed.

"I'd tell you that you're beautiful, but it seems like such a dull word."

"All the admiration I need is reflected in your expression," she whispered back. She lightly rested a hand on his sleeve. Her soft floral scent teased his nose with every movement; she was much the personification of spring. "I rather thought this day would never come, but alternately, the time has flown so quickly."

"Indeed, it has."

The clergyman grinned. "Shall we begin?" To the guests, he said, "The bridal pair would like to start; they are quite anxious."

Murmurs and tittering laughter buzzed through the room as everyone found chairs. Even his mother attended the ceremony.

Then Mr. Anders nodded. He included them both in his gaze. "Please face me." When they did, he looked past them and opened his book to the appropriate page. "Dearly beloved, we are gathered together here in the sight of God, and in the face of these witnesses, to join together this man and this woman in holy matrimony; which is an honorable estate, instituted of God in the time of man's innocency, signifying unto us the mystical union that is betwixt Christ and his Church…"

Cornelius had difficulty focusing on the clergyman's words, for the whole of his concentration rested upon the woman at his side. Dear God, after all this time, he would say vows to her and begin their life together. No longer was she merely a dream. She turned her head and met his gaze with a soft smile. He returned the gesture and then gave his attention to the clergyman.

The man continued, his voice a pleasing timbre as he talked about the holy state they were about to embark upon. He held the prayer book in his hands, the brown leather spine cracked and worn, while he addressed Cornelius. "Wilt thou have this woman to thy wedded wife, to live together after God's ordinance in the holy estate of matrimony?" His lips curved with a smile, as if he already knew what the answer would be. "Wilt thou love her, comfort her, honor her, and keep her in sickness and in health; and, forsaking all others, keep thee only unto her, so long as ye both shall live?"

"I most certainly will." He peered at Penny and flashed the grin he hoped would forever charm her. "She has always been my ideal."

"I'm quite certain none of us here doubt your words," Mr. Anders said. Indulgent chuckles circled through the gathered guests. Then he addressed Penny. "Wilt thou have this man to thy wedded husband, to live together after God's ordinance in the holy estate of matrimony? Wilt thou obey him, and serve him, love him, honor him, and keep him in sickness and in health; and, forsaking all others, keep thee only unto him, so long as ye both shall live?"

"I will." Penny's voice never wavered. "I have long looked forward to this day, ever since he was my crush before I ever understood what love truly was or entailed."

A few of the ladies present sighed.

"I rather suspected that answer." Mr. Anders instructed Cornelius to take her right hand in his right, which he then did, and Penny's hand shook. Was she nervous or merely excited? Surely, she knew he would always protect her and strive to build a pleasant life with him. "Major Montgomery, please repeat after me…"

With solicitous attention, Cornelius tried to memorize the handful of words and then uttered them aloud. "I, Cornelius Thomas Montgomery, take thee Lady Penelope Anne Needham nee Wilmington as my wedded wife, to have and to hold from this day forward, for better for worse, for richer for poorer, in sickness and in health, to love and to cherish, until death us do part…" His throat tightened as he spoke those most sacred of words that would forever bind him with her. "… according to God's holy ordinance; and thereto I plight thee my troth."

My wife. She will soon be my wife. What have I done right in my life to win her?

Mr. Anders nodded. "Please release hands. Major, take her left in your left hand." Once they'd done as instructed, with the braided hair ring still on his finger, he trained his attention on Penny. "Lady Penelope, repeat after me." He gave her the words, much like the ones he'd said to Cornelius moments before.

The delicate tendons in her neck moved with a heavy swallow, but she found his gaze. "I, Lady Penelope Anne Needham nee Wilmington take thee Major Cornelius Thomas Montgomery as my wedded husband." Her voice broke on the last word. A sheen of tears made her eyes luminous and bright, but he squeezed her fingers, and she continued. "To have and to hold from this day forward, for better for worse, for richer, for poorer, in sickness and in health, to love, cherish, and to obey, until death us do part, according to God's holy ordinance." A tear fell to her cheek, but her dazzling smile let him know she wasn't in distress. "And thereto I give thee my troth."

"It is lovely when a nuptial ceremony is steeped in emotion." Mr. Anders grinned. Lines framed his eyes and mouth. "Please release your hands." To Cornelius, he whispered, "Now is the time to offer up a ring and any respects you might have for my services."

"Ah, thank you for the reminder. It's not every day a man marries." Chuckles circled about the room while Cornelius dug the ring from the pocket of his waistcoat, which he gave to the clergyman, who rested it upon his open *Book of Common Prayer*. He followed it with a small leather pouch as payment and gratuity for services rendered.

"I appreciate it." Mr. Anders returned the ring to Cornelius. "You may present the ring to the lady." As soon as he slipped it onto the fourth finger of Penny's left hand, the clergyman spoke again, the words directed to him. "Please repeat after me."

A shudder went down his spine, for a woman had finally managed to bring him up to scratch, and he looked forward to being domesticated. He held Penny's gaze and rejoiced in the happiness in those blue-gray pools. "With this ring I thee wed, with my body I thee worship, and with all my worldly goods I thee endow. In the name of the Father, and of the Son, and of the Holy Ghost. Amen." Then he raised her hand to his lips and kissed the ring he'd just put onto her finger. The center diamond winked, and the tiny round sapphires that surrounded the larger stone glittered like mad in the sunlight. It was perfectly nestled against the silver band he'd given her years ago.

Mr. Anders nodded. "Please kneel while everyone is invited to pray with me."

As the words of the prayer flowed over him, Cornelius dared to peek at Penny. She looked back at him with a serene smile curving her lips, and a shiver of anticipation went down his spine. *God, I can't wait to claim her as her husband.* Then the prayer was over, and Cornelius stood. He smoothly brought Penny to her feet.

The clergyman closed his book. "I now pronounce thee husband and wife. May your union be long and happy."

Applause broke out among the gathered guests.

Cornelius turned, as did she, and he caught her hand in his. "I can finally call you my wife," he whispered to her, but she couldn't reply as people surged forward and offered congratulations and murmured well-wishes. He stood back to watch her interact with their friends and guests. She was as elegant and gracious as a duchess, and he couldn't believe she was his.

Will she discover the truth and know I'm woefully below her?

Then a new thought occurred that chilled his blood. What if what he offered her wasn't enough? Would she look elsewhere for fulfillment?

"You're worried," she said from his side as she slipped her arm through his. "Why? This is the day we've both wanted for years."

He glanced at her, caught the compassion in her gaze, and fell into those cool pools. "You deserve a man so much more than I am, deserve more than I'll be able to give. I am—"

"Simply perfect for me." She briefly rolled her gaze to the ceiling before focusing on him once more. "I will never tire of you. Neither will I complain about the style in which I'm kept for none of that is as important than who we are together."

"You won't change your mind a few years into the marriage?" A knot of anxiety pulled in his belly. "I've married you for nothing other than love. What if that isn't enough?"

"It is enough and more, so stop stewing. I'll not change my mind." With a gentle tug on his arm, she led him across the room. While he'd been mentally dithering, the guests had gone, probably to partake of an excellent wedding breakfast being served in the dining room. Even Mr. Anders had exited the room. "However, there *is* something you can do for me right now."

"What?"

She halted their forward movement, turned into him, and slid her hands up his chest. "I want you to kiss me." Though the look in her eyes gave off a blatant come-hither air, the wobble of her chin spoke to a vulnerability and emotion, perhaps due to the ordeal of planning for the wedding. "I've waited so long, and not being able to touch you has nearly driven me mad."

His worries melted away as he took her into his arms. "I know exactly how you've felt." With a sigh, he pressed his lips to hers, and just like the other times when he'd kissed her, a match went to tinder and started an inferno. He pulled slightly away, searching her face, and when the tip of her tongue swiped her bottom lip, he groaned. One hand moved to the back of her neck while the other he curled about her hip as he crushed his mouth to hers.

For the next several seconds he reacquainted himself with every centimeter of her lips, memorized the curve of the bottom one, nibbled at the corners. When she whimpered, he realized it wasn't enough; he needed so much more. He deepened the kiss, sought out her tongue with his until they dueled and fought for dominance. Need streaked through his body, and he held her ever closer so she'd feel the evidence of his desire. Finally, she was his, and he didn't care if there were twenty people in her brother's house; he wanted her now.

Penny wrenched away. Her kiss-swollen lips curved in a smile. "You haven't lost your potency, Major." The words were a trifle breathless.

"Neither have you, my lady, or rather Mrs. Montgomery, should you wish to use that moniker." Oh, how sweet that sounded! "Perhaps we should join our well-wishers lest I claim you right here in the drawing room. And we do need to sign the register." If his voice was a tad shaky, there was good reason. This was his wedding day, and she was his.

"We do, but it can wait until after breakfast."

"And by the by, I'm imagining you naked wearing nothing except your rings."

Her eyes darkened with desire. She laughed, and the smokey sound worked to further his undoing. "That can be arranged, for it has been far too long since I've seen you without clothes."

Then she shook her head. "I'm famished due to not having an appetite for a few days."

Immediately concerned, he frowned. "Are you well?"

"I am, but there is something I wish to say to you before we meet with our guests." She rested a hand on his chest, fiddled with his cravat as a blush colored her cheeks. "Yesterday, I managed to slip away from both Mama and Johnathan on an errand, where I went to a midwife, who I met through one of my charities."

"Oh?" As his knees felt far too weak, he wished he'd grabbed his cane before he'd been carried away with kissing his new wife. "And?" He could hardly speak for anticipation and worry.

"And, since I've missed my menses for two months ever since you and I first came together, and I haven't felt my best this past week or so, I wanted the midwife's opinion." The delicate tendons of her neck worked with a hard swallow. "She performed an examination, and she told me that I'm a bit over two months pregnant. We most likely created this child the first time we shared intercourse, which makes that time even more special." Tears filled her eyes. "I'm increasing, Cornelius. You will be a father in late November."

"What?" Though he staggered backward a few steps, he immediately came back to her and put his hands at her hips. "You are... are..."

"I am." She nodded with a soft grin and tears on her cheeks. "It's also why I haven't had an appetite and why certain smells have bothered me of late." With a palm against his cheek, she asked, "You *are* happy about this, aren't you?"

"Happy doesn't even begin to describe what I'm feeling." With a loud whoop of smug victory, he lifted her off her feet and then twirled her about in circles. "I'm quite convinced I've never known what joy was like until this moment." When he finally set her on the floor again, he kissed her and put so much emotion behind that gesture, he hoped she would know everything he said was the truth.

"I'm so glad." She nestled into his arms and sighed as he held her close. "I was bereft when this couldn't happen while I was with Weymouth, but it seems all too right that it's happening now, with you."

"It truly does." Waves of happiness poured over him, and Cornelius couldn't help but press a kiss to the top of her head. "I'm afraid I don't know what to do with myself or how to act or even what to say." Yet the second he met her gaze, a sense of calm came over him. "I love you."

"I love you too." For long moments, they remained like that, both reveling in everything the day had brought. Eventually, she stirred. "Let's go into breakfast. The sooner we do, the sooner we can retire to our home."

Home.

How long had it been since he'd felt he truly had a place where he belonged? "And to our nuptial bed." A quick gasp escaped him. "Will such wicked things harm the babe?"

"I shouldn't think so. My midwife said it was perfectly natural." She stepped from the circle of his arms then grasped his hand. "This is the second-best day of my life."

He frowned. "Not the first?"

"No."

"Why?"

"Because the first one was the afternoon you came into Mr. Chandler's bookshop to bedevil me with charming words and your kisses. I knew then you would completely upend my life."

"And you've done the same to mine." He brought her hand to his lips and kissed the back. "Thank God for that. I fear I was stagnating before."

There was much to look forward to, and never once did he give thought to the life he'd led before she'd come back into his life. Those days were well and truly behind him, and he didn't miss them at all. Not while there was a different sort of excitement ahead.

EPILOGUE

February 14, 1819
No. 10
Manchester Square
Marylebone, London

CORNELIUS CAME INTO the rooms he shared with his wife that evening with a bouquet of hothouse flowers in hand. "Penny, the carriage has been called. It's nearly time. If we don't leave now, we'll be late for your brother's engagement ball."

Interesting, that, for Birchfield had finally sorted himself enough that he'd allowed himself to find a romance of his own. Apparently, it had happened during Christmastide the year before, and he'd kept it quite secret for fear that things might be jinxed. Not that Cornelius could blame him. Love was a funny and fickle, quite like fate, and when a man was caught up in it, he often wondered if it was real.

He couldn't be happier for his best, for there had been times when he thought he might lose him over the years. It was far too difficult to pull oneself out of the dark places the mind decided to tread after trauma, but the earl had done it, with the help of his now fiancée.

As he came into the dressing room, his wife of nearly two years emerged from behind the silk privacy screen painted with vines and delicate spring flowers. Though the gown she wore of a dark-red satin suited her complexion and showed her form to perfection, her face was far too pale for his liking.

"Is all well?" he asked upon noting the folded handkerchief she pressed to her mouth and came further into the room.

"Yes, I believe so. Just a bit of an upset stomach." But when she met his gaze, something deep in the blue-gray depths alerted him that there was more.

"My darling girl, when will you realize that you can't lie to me? I know you far too well?" After placing the floral bouquet on a small, rose-inlaid table, Cornelius crossed the room to his wife and took her hands. "Tell me. Are you ill? Worried? Is something wrong with Nathaniel?"

Their son was fifteen months old, and he was the most adorable child, already so clever and bright and developing a sense of humor. He had the blue-gray eyes of his mother but Cornelius's hair, except the boy's tended to curl, and he had the most adorable dimple in his left cheek. Easily, the child was the miracle of his life, and he constantly doted on him.

"Nathaniel is simply lovely," she said as she came into his arms with a tiny sigh. "He is upstairs with his nurse and nanny, no doubt dreaming of whatever it is that babies dream about." The depths of her eyes held secrets and shadows and the wages of experience. "However, I remember this sickness; I endured it when I was carrying him."

He uttered a small gasp. "Does this mean…?"

"I think it might." She rested a palm against his chest, but her smile was bittersweet. "After we lost our last pregnancy, I couldn't bear to hope, but this one feels different. The sickness is strong where I had none with the last one."

A wealth of emotions flooded him, but he tucked her into his arms and encouraged Penny to rest her head on his shoulder. "When will you know for certain?"

"I'll ask the midwife to call sometime this week."

Unaccountable joy came over him. "Another baby. I'm so in awe of you." Losing the other one last year had been a dark time for them both, but Nathaniel had kept their spirits up and reminded them that miracles did happen. "It's a wonderful thing."

"It is."

"If you don't wish to go to your brother's ball tonight…"

"No, I do." She pulled back in order to peer up into his face. "I've been looking forward to it, and his fiancée is such an interesting woman. And Mama is beside herself with joy."

"I'll wager she is." Having a married daughter with a child and now, finally, her son had taken up the reins of his responsibilities. "You should be resting."

"Pish posh, Major." With a playful smack to his arm, she tucked the handkerchief into a clever pocket sewn into the folds of her skirt. "I'm well enough to attend an event for a few hours." She searched his face with her gaze. "Are you happy about having another child? Unless I miss my guess, this one will arrive in September."

"Sweeting, I'm over the moon but concerned about your health." He rested his forehead against hers. "We might need to move to a slightly larger house."

She nodded. "I look forward to it, as long as we remain in this same area. It's a lovely place to raise children. We still have the money left to me from my first marriage, and if need be, I can sell some of the parures. Thank goodness Weymouth's will specifically noted that he'd left those to me instead of allowing his brother to inherit them. Nothing is as valuable to me as the health and happiness of you and our growing family."

"I feel the same." He nodded. "What of your bookshop?" A few months after they'd married, she'd met another dream of hers and opened a dear little bookshop in Mayfair called Pages and Quills, where she happily worked around the responsibilities of motherhood and the charities she supported.

As for him, he had a string of speaking engagements throughout the year at various clubs and organizations. His speeches centered around enduring hardship and keeping a stiff upper lip in the face of obstacles, and though it wasn't the most fulfilling of duties, it kept him busy and forced him out of the house to mingle with society, when he wasn't spending his time with his son.

"What of it? Books will endure. I shall simply hire another clerk to assist when I can't be there due to other commitments."

"It truly seems as if we are living our dreams." He cupped her cheek. "Thank you, for giving me all of this. I never thought it possible before you."

"Neither did I." When she grinned, his world tilted as it always did when she was near. "You are a good man, Cornelius, but then, I've always thought so."

Slipping his hand to her nape, he gently drew her closer then claimed her lips with his. After a few moments spent kissing his wife, he released her. "We should probably go. This is Birchfield's grand celebration; I'd hate to miss it."

She nodded. "I'm happy for my brother. Perhaps our children will have cousins to play with."

"Imagine that." As he escorted his wife from the room, Cornelius couldn't help but grin. It was miraculous, really, and quite mysterious how the love of a woman could completely change a man's life and priorities. When that happened, the difficult days didn't seem so bad after all, for there was always something to look forward to.

And he was damned fortunate, indeed.

The End

About the Author

Sandra Sookoo is a *USA Today* bestselling author who firmly believes every person deserves acceptance and a happy ending. Most days you can find her creating scandal and mischief in the Regency-era, serendipity and happenstance in Victorian America or snarky, sweet humor in the contemporary world. Most recently she's moved into infusing her books with mystery and intrigue. Reading is a lot like eating fine chocolates—you can't just have one. Good thing books don't have calories!

When she's not wearing out computer keyboards, Sandra spends time with her real-life Prince Charming in central Indiana where she's been known to goof off and make moments count because the key to life is laughter. A Disney fan since the age of ten, when her soul gets bogged down and her imagination flags, a trip to Walt Disney World is in order. Nothing fuels her dreams more than the land of eternal happy endings, hope and love stories.

Stay in Touch

Sign up for Sandra's bi-monthly newsletter and you'll be given exclusive excerpts, cover reveals before the general public as well as opportunities to enter contests you won't find anywhere else.

Just send an email to sandrasookoo@yahoo.com with SUB-SCRIBE in the subject line.

Or follow/friend her on social media:
Facebook: facebook.com/sandra.sookoo
Facebook Author Page: facebook.com/sandrasookooauthor
Pinterest: pinterest.com/sandrasookoo
Instagram: instagram.com/sandrasookoo
BookBub Page: bookbub.com/authors/sandra-sookoo